GUSTAV GLOOM

AND THE FOUR TERRORS

S0-AAD-435

by Adam-Troy Castro
illustrated by Kristen Margiotta

Grosset & Dunlap
An Imprint of Penguin Group (USA) LLC

GROSSET & DUNLAP
Published by the Penguin Group
Penguin Group (USA) LLC, 375 Hudson Street, New York, New York 10014, USA

USA | Canada | UK | Ireland | Australia | New Zealand | India | South Africa | China

penguin.com
A Penguin Random House Company

Text copyright © 2013 by Adam-Troy Castro. Illustrations copyright © 2013 by
Kristen Margiotta. All rights reserved. Published by Grosset & Dunlap, a division
of Penguin Young Readers Group, 345 Hudson Street, New York, New York 10014.
This paperback edition published in 2014. GROSSET & DUNLAP is a trademark
of Penguin Group (USA) LLC. Manufactured in China.

Book design by Christina Quintero. Typeset in MrsEaves, Neutraface,
and Strangelove Text.

The Library of Congress has cataloged the hardcover edition under the following
Control Number: 2012025517

ISBN 978-0-448-48330-6   10 9 8 7 6 5 4 3 2 1

This one's for Morgan and Megan

CHAPTER ONE
THE WOMAN WHO PUT SWEATERS ON DUCKS

For the fourth time in two days, Mrs. Zoe Soggybottom yelled, "No! Stop! Wait!"

The front door of the Fluorescent Salmon house on Sunnyside Terrace burst open, and the young couple she'd been giving the grand tour lurched into the afternoon sun.

Panic had turned the man and woman different colors. The man was as red as a beet, and the woman as pale as the underbelly of a frog. Fear had contorted both of their mouths into shapes like coin slots.

They stumbled down the driveway to the compact car with the bumper sticker assuring everybody unimpressed with their vehicle that their other car was a far more expensive one.

As they ran, a small mob of angry gray shapes clung to their shoulders and shouted in their ears. Two of those shapes were the shadows of little girls; another was the shadow of a house cat, inflated to giant size and roaring with the ferocity of India's grumpiest tiger.

Some of the dark shapes shouted things like "Get out!" and "Go away!" and "Go live in some other Fluorescent Salmon house!"

The man and woman dove into their compact car and pulled out in a hurry, knocking over both the mailbox and the lawn sign reading HOME FOR SALE: OPEN HOUSE. The car squealed as it veered across the narrow street. Its rear bumper hopped the sidewalk on the other side and smashed into a black iron fence that surrounded the yard of an ominous, sprawling old mansion.

The rolling mist that covered the yard sprouted its own small army of dark shapes, protesting this attack on their domain. "Whoa!" shouted one. "Hey!" said another. "Watch where you're going!" cried a third.

The woman screamed the same five words over and over, without any pause for breath between them. It sounded like "GETUSOUT OFHEREGETUSOUTOFHEREGETUSOUT OFHERE." This wasn't the kind of thing likely to improve her husband's driving. He accelerated too fast and turned too sloppily. The car hopped the curb on its driver's-side wheels and rode half on and half off the grass, knocking down mailboxes and drawing a deep rut in the lawns as it went.

Somewhere along the way the man realized that he needed to avoid a car parked against the curb. He corrected in the wrong direction, leaving a pair of tire tracks on the lawn belonging to one Mrs. Adele Everwiner. After clipping the rear bumper of her car, his car hopped back off the curb and onto the street, still picking up speed as it vanished around the curve.

The shadows responsible for chasing the young couple from the Fluorescent Salmon house slid back across the driveway and toward the front door, congratulating one another on their fine performance.

The one shaped like the smaller of the two girls met up with a real flesh-and-blood girl now appearing at the front door: freckle-faced, curly-haired, ten-year-old Fernie.

"That," she declared, "was the best one yet."

As she reclaimed her own shadow, Fernie's twelve-year-old sister, Pearlie, worried. "It may have been a bit much this time. Look at all the damage. Dad's going to throw a fit."

Fernie stuck out her lower lip. "It's not our fault that the people looking for houses nowadays are all a bunch of cowardly wusses."

Harrington, the family's beloved black-and-white cat, appeared at their feet, feasting his golden-green eyes on the epic destruction before him. He sniffed the nose of his own shadow, which had shrunk back down to a manageable cat size but was not yet ready to calm down and behave. His plaintive meow might have been Cat for "Nice work. I would have helped out, but I saw that you had the situation fully under control."

The shadow Harrington meowed back. *Sure you did.*

Zoe Soggybottom reached the front door behind them, her hazel eyes as round as dinner plates. Zoe was a tall, fussy woman with a weak chin and a beak of a nose that, between them, made her face look like it had been designed to come to a point. She wore the official red pantsuit of Lucky Lemon Realtors, complete with a bright yellow lapel pin promising WE SELL THE HOUSES NO ONE ELSE CAN!

She looked pale. "Why is everybody doing that?"

"Doing what?" Fernie asked, even though she knew the answer very well.

"Running away."

"I don't think it's anything you said," Fernie replied.

"They didn't like the sunroom," Pearlie suggested.

"Or maybe it's a problem with the backyard," Fernie ventured. "It's not even close to being big enough for a pool."

Mrs. Soggybottom looked faint. "I'm not sure that explains all the screaming and panicking and fleeing for their lives."

"Well," Fernie said, "maybe that's because the ad in the paper is attracting too many nervous people. Maybe instead of calling the house a 'sunny little family home in a high-end neighborhood,' you should call it a 'perfect home for thrill-seekers eager to challenge the unknown.' You know. Get some braver types to look at the place."

Mrs. Soggybottom flashed the girls an uncomprehending smile before drifting back inside to flutter around the kitchen counter like a blind moth.

The two What girls glanced at each other,

each a little ashamed about how they were treating the poor woman. They liked Mrs. Soggybottom, really. She had a warm smile, a fine sense of humor, and (as she'd explained at length, between tours of their house) a deep commitment to her personal charity, a volunteer group that knit waterproof sweaters for ducks. Her pet cause didn't make any more sense to the girls than it likely did to the ducks, but it demonstrated that the lady had her heart in the right place.

Unfortunately, she was also trying to sell the house for their father, and neither the What girls nor the various shadows of the household could permit that to happen.

The girls retreated to Pearlie's bedroom, which was decorated on one side with pictures of giant monsters busily making buildings collapse, and on the other with posters of a popular boy singer who had the same effect on girls.

Pearlie murmured, "I'm not sure how long we can keep this up."

"We're not doing anything," Fernie declared. "We can't help it if our shadows are misbehaving."

"They're only misbehaving because we asked them to."

"And we only asked them to because we have to. It's only until we come up with a better idea."

"But what if there is no better idea?" Pearlie worried aloud. "Scaring people away isn't going to solve the problem forever. Sooner or later Dad's going to move us away just because he wants to, whether he sells the house or not."

This was true. Mr. What was a world-renowned safety expert, famous for cataloging over a thousand terrible things that could happen when spatulas were hung on insufficiently secured hooks. He made a living out of taking positions like declaring the need for warning sirens on grocery carts. He had not taken well to learning that the house across the street contained a gateway to a place called the Dark Country, where all shadows come from, or having his beloved daughters exposed to mortal danger two times in less than a month.

What the What girls needed was a way to change his mind. But they had no idea how.

They were still considering this when another dark shape slid into the room and settled against the nearest wall. "Hello, girls."

From prior meetings, Fernie recognized the shape as a shadow that had once belonged to a not very nice man named Mr. Notes, until deciding several years earlier to live apart from him. "Hello, Mr. Notes. Sorry about what happened to your fence."

"Don't worry about it, Fernie. We'll fix it. But Gustav sent me over because there is something important he needs to discuss. Can you get away long enough to meet him?"

"Sure," Fernie said. "Tell him we're coming."

Mr. Notes's shadow flitted away to deliver the message.

Mr. What had forbidden the girls from ever braving the dangers of the Gloom estate again, or even spending any time in its front yard, but had out of kindness said that they were still allowed to meet their good friend Gustav at his fence. The alternative was not to see him again at all, because Gustav started to give off smoke the second he left the confines of the Gloom estate. Friends had to go to him; he couldn't ever go to them.

On their way out, the two girls found Mrs. Soggybottom slumped on the sofa, looking defeated. As her frightened eyes searched the room's four corners for mysterious moving shapes, she seemed less like somebody who was supposed to be there than somebody who had landed there after falling from a height.

Fernie wondered if they'd gone too far. "Ummm, Mrs. Soggybottom? We're going to go see our friend across the street, but we'll be right back."

"Sure," Mrs. Soggybottom said a little foggily. "Don't do anything I wouldn't do."

Wondering what that could possibly mean, the two girls crossed Sunnyside Terrace and found their friend Gustav standing behind the iron fence, gripping the bars in his pale white hands. The ankle-deep mist that always billowed around his property obscured his shiny black shoes, but they matched his little black suit with the little red tie, each as dark as his sun-deprived skin was pale. He wasn't alone, because Mr. Notes's shadow stood with him. But when the shadow saw that the girls were coming, he sank back down into the mist, disappearing from view.

The dark circles under Gustav's eyes were more pronounced than usual today, suggesting either a lack of sleep or worries unusual even for a boy who had spent his entire life dealing with the many strange challenges of life inside the Gloom house. "Hello, Fernie, Pearlie. I see the sale's not going well."

"It's never going to go well," Fernie declared. "We're not leaving you."

"I appreciate that," said Gustav, who really did seem to. "I hope you don't get into too much trouble with your dad because of it. If my dad were around, I wouldn't want to be in any trouble with him."

Fernie felt guilty. "It would have been okay. You can't be a kid without getting into trouble with your parents every once in a while."

"It's part of the point of being a kid," Pearlie emphasized.

"If you have parents," said Gustav, which made Fernie feel even worse. "I wouldn't know."

Gustav's human mother had been killed by a bad man named Howard Philip October, and his mother's shadow, who'd raised him in her stead, had disappeared without explanation years later. He still had a living father, but poor Hans Gloom had been trapped in the Dark Country since before Gustav was born, a prisoner of Howard Philip October, the villain now known as Lord Obsidian.

Now Gustav said, "That's why I've decided that it's time I rescue my dad."

This announcement stunned the girls.

Fernie asked him, "Won't you have to go to the Dark Country to do that?"

"The problem with having to rescue people," Gustav pointed out, "is that you pretty much always have to go wherever they are."

"Yes." Pearlie sighed. "It would be much more convenient if people could rescue people without ever leaving our houses."

Gustav looked confused. "Really? I've rescued you once and Fernie twice without ever leaving my house, and I wouldn't call it convenient at all."

This also happened to be true.

"Anyway," he said, getting back on track, "I need some help preparing for the trip. It's something that only Fernie can do, and that can only be done inside my house."

Fernie hesitated. After everything they'd been through with Gustav, it would be horrible to refuse him, but she couldn't see any good way to say yes without disobeying her dad. "I'm not sure I could get away with that, Gustav."

But Gustav seemed to have thought of this

already. "Don't worry. I like your dad a lot. I don't think there's any reason to go behind his back. Why don't you let me talk to him when he gets home? I think I have a plan that even he'll agree to."

Pearlie was dubious. "It'll have to be a really, *really* good plan, Gustav."

"That's okay," Gustav said complacently. "I'm good at coming up with really, *really* good plans."

This was something Fernie knew to be true, even if a plan capable of satisfying her father would have to be more than just really, *really* good; it would have to be brilliant. "All right," she said. "It's up to you, then. We'll tell him as soon as he gets home."

Of course, almost as soon as she said this, Mr. What's car inched around the corner, the head of a honking line of other cars that wanted to pass him but couldn't because he was driving in the middle of the road at a speed slower than a walk.

As the cars drew close enough for the girls to hear some of the nasty names the other drivers were shouting out their car windows, Mr. What's eyes widened at the tire tracks gouged in the previously immaculate green lawns.

"This is *so* not going to be good," fretted Pearlie.

Mr. What turned into his driveway, beside the car belonging to Mrs. Zoe Soggybottom. The cars he'd trapped seized the chance to escape and zoomed past the house all in a rush, their drivers shouting a few more choice insults out their windows. Mr. What didn't seem to hear them, but instead could only stare at the trail of destruction.

Mr. What was a gentle man, with a soft face dominated by a pair of black eyeglasses too big for his head. Yelling at his daughters did not come easily to him. Mostly, when they did something wrong, he calmly explained why it had been wrong and was so reasonable about it that they didn't have the heart to argue.

But whenever they misbehaved so badly that even he had to yell, he seemed to grow an extra pair of lungs for additional volume. "PEARLIEEEEE! FERNIEEEEEE! I WANT TO TALK TO YOU *NOW*!"

Behind the fence, Gustav grew paler. "Of course, it's also perfectly okay if we wait for the right time."

CHAPTER TWO
THE LEAST HELPFUL BUTLER IN THE WORLD

Mr. What told the girls that he was leaving with Mrs. Soggybottom to straighten things out with her boss, and that he had better find them in their rooms when he got back.

This would have been a quick errand for anybody who drove at a normal rate of speed. But by the time Mr. What's car came back around the same bend leading another parade of honking drivers, the setting sun had disappeared behind the rooftops and the first stars had begun to discuss the possibility of showing themselves for the evening.

The girls, who had left their separate rooms within thirty seconds of his departure and had stationed themselves at the living room window to keep an eye out for his return, were watching when he got out of his car, and therefore witnessed what had to be the most exasperating part of his day: a confrontation with their neighbor Mrs. Adele Everwiner, who had seen the damage to her lawn and wanted to give him a piece of her mind.

Mrs. Everwiner spent so much of her life giving people a piece of her mind that it was a small miracle she had any pieces left.

When the mostly round Mrs. Everwiner confronted the stick-thin Mr. What, the argument looked like the number 0 trying to frighten the number 1. She was carrying her nasty little dog, Snooks 5, and wearing one of her more colorful outfits, a frock exactly the same shade of green that comes out of a runny nose, behind a pattern of aggressively yellow sunflowers. Whenever she waved her arms at him, which she did a lot, the design looked like a windstorm wreaking havoc in a meadow.

For a while Mr. What seemed to get out only a word at a time, every thirty seconds or so. Then he seemed to gain control of the conversation and said quite a bit, all at once, his eyebrows knitting together in the way they did on the rare occasions when he was angry. He pointed at her, not just once but three times. She reared back each time, as if expecting a mouth at the end of that finger to open up like the jaws of a poisonous snake and bite her.

Whatever he wound up with for his big finish was so devastating that she threw her head back and marched away, her perfect cone of scarlet hair pointing into the air like a big loaf of French bread sticking out of a grocery bag.

Fernie and Pearlie ran back to their rooms and were both where their father had told them they had better be when he got back. This, as far as they were concerned, amounted to obeying him, since he had told them, "You'd better be in your rooms when I get back" and not "You'd better stay in your rooms until I get back," which is a different instruction entirely.

The door slammed. "Fernie! Pearlie! You get into the living room *now!*"

In a flash the girls appeared before him, leading Harrington, who liked to be involved in all family discussions.

Mr. What held on to his angry face for only a couple of seconds before his expression softened and he collapsed onto the living room couch, looking defeated. Without a word, the girls sat on either side of him, each taking one of his hands and resting a head on one of his shoulders.

"You know," he said after a few seconds, "there's a good reason I've never let you go on any of your mother's expeditions."

Mrs. What was a famous adventurer who was usually off filming TV specials of her doing things like skiing down sheer cliffs.

"You think they're too dangerous for us," Pearlie said.

Mr. What surprised them both. "No, that's not it. It's not that I don't think you'd enjoy swimming with crocodiles or kayaking over waterfalls; it's that I never thought there was much point to letting you take such crazy risks unless I first taught you how to stay safe, so you had something to compare it to."

"You mean you'd be okay with us going on an adventure with Mom?"

"I'm going to put that day off as long as I can," he said sadly, "but I know I won't be able to control everything you do forever. You both take after your mom so much more than you take after me, and you'll be out having adventures soon enough. Maybe if you were both big old scaredy-cats like me, hiding from every danger that came along, I'd feel better about you two living across the street from the Gloom house.

But you're both risk takers, and I can't be sure that you'll always stay out of danger if you have a choice. We *have to* sell the house."

The girls recognized that their father had as difficult a problem as their own.

Then Fernie realized something. "Dad? If you're right about that, wouldn't living here be just as dangerous to anybody else who moved in?"

Mr. What smiled slightly, the way all fathers do when their children ask naive questions. He opened his mouth to provide her with the benefits of his parental wisdom, and then shut it just as quickly, his confident smile fading.

"If you really think living across the street

c   e is too dangerous," she

f   is it okay to let another

           of chagrin was now a

g   aight line from one side

c   er. "I . . . don't know."

           ming from you than it

w   anybody else who sold

th   're such a world-famous

sa   xpect you to tell the truth about what's safe and what's not. You can't sell a house to somebody else if you think it's too dangerous to live in. You just can't."

Some successful arguments are like heavy meals, filling you up so completely that you barely have enough energy to move. Fernie's argument had precisely this effect on Mr. What.

Clinging to his other arm, Pearlie suggested, "Fernie, maybe you should tell him the other part."

It wasn't the right time yet, according to Fernie's calculations, especially not with Mr. What turning pale at the very thought of his day choosing this moment to get even more complicated.

Almost afraid, he said, "What? Why? What else have you done?"

Fernie had spent the last few hours trying to figure out how to trick her dad into agreeing to meet with Gustav . . . but realized now that she'd failed to consider just telling him the truth. "Gustav said he wanted to talk to you about something."

All the fear went out of Mr. What's face at once, now that he had a simple problem he knew how to deal with. "When did he say that?"

"Just before you came home earlier this afternoon."

Mr. What jumped to his feet right away. "And you waited this long to tell me? Girls, that was rude. We'd better go and see what he needs."

It was that simple. Mr. What may have had a problem with Gustav's house, but he had never had a problem with Gustav himself. He'd said many times that he *liked* Gustav.

Mr. What led his daughters out the front door of the What house and across the street to the Gloom estate. Fernie thought that he would abide by the same restrictions he'd declared for the girls and not advance any farther than the iron fence, but instead he opened the gate and marched through like any general leading a charge against enemy lines. By the time he knocked on the house's giant front doors—the same seven knocks he always used on doors, that went along with a nursery chant about a shave and a haircut—the girls were both a little ashamed of how completely they'd underestimated him.

When the door opened, Fernie expected to see one of the shadows she knew, like Mr. Notes or Great-Aunt Mellifluous, but instead saw a hulking gray figure in a black tuxedo. His face was covered in little spots identical to those the girls had sprouted during their bad week with chicken pox. The long entrance hallway, lined with portraits and vases, stretched far behind him, the long red carpet runner extending all the way to the cavernous grand parlor at the house's center.

"Yes?" he intoned.

Mr. What stepped back. "I didn't know this house had a butler."

"A fine house this would be," the shadow replied disdainfully, "without a butler."

"I'm sorry," Mr. What said. "I'm just surprised, that's all. We've never met you before. I'm Mr. What. I live across the street. These are my daughters, Pearlie and Fernie. We're friends of Gustav."

"None of this is information I need to have," said the shadow butler. "Is that all?"

"Why, no. We'd like to see Gustav, if he's available."

"Seeing the boy if he was *not* available," the shadow butler droned, "would be an even more impressive trick, would it not?"

Mr. What chuckled nervously. "Yes, that's a good point. But we'd still like to see Gustav."

The shadow butler nodded. "Please stay here."

He closed the door.

They waited a long time.

After a few minutes, time started crawling, and the girls began shifting their weight from one side to the other.

"This is ridiculous," Pearlie contributed.

"We can't be sure of that," Mr. What said. "These people may not keep regular hours. Maybe they're all in bed or something."

"I don't think they sleep," said Fernie. "I don't think even *Gustav* sleeps."

"Come on," Pearlie protested. "He has to."

"I don't know," Fernie said, "but he always seems to be dressed up in that little black suit of his at all hours of the day or night. I came here long after midnight that first time and spent the whole night the second time, and I didn't seem to be interrupting his bedtime at all."

"I could use the same argument," Pearlie pointed out, "to prove that you don't sleep, either."

"I can't believe I'm hearing this," Mr. What mourned, "from the two girls who woke me up at four A.M. a couple of months ago by having a game of tag in my living room. I don't think *any* of you kids need sleep."

Several minutes passed. The impatient sighs from the What girls began to overwhelm the time between sighs.

Mr. What announced, "I know it's a big house, but if he's not back in another minute or so, I'm going to knock again."

That minute passed, exactly like the ones before it.

Mr. What knocked again, using the same shave-and-a-haircut rhythm.

The door opened a second time, revealing the same cold, contemptuous figure. He rolled his eyes in contempt when he saw the Whats still on the front stoop, waiting for him. "Yes?"

"I'm sorry," Mr. What began, "but we were beginning to think you weren't coming back."

"I wasn't," the shadow butler said.

"But you told us to wait—"

"No, I did not. I told you to *stay there*. That is not the same thing as promising to carry your message or come back with that intolerable boy, neither of which I intend to do unless I'm specifically ordered to. Otherwise, it's just something I said to keep you satisfied while I did neither of those things. Would you still like me to go get Gustav?"

Before Fernie or Pearlie could stop him, Mr. What said, "Yes, please."

"Fine," the shadow butler said. "Stay here."

He closed the door on them again.

The girls cried, *"Daddy!"*

"I know," Mr. What said with chagrin. "I hope they don't pay him much."

He knocked on the door yet again with the shave-and-a-haircut refrain.

The door opened a third time, the unhelpful shadow butler with the spotted face looking even more displeased to see them. "Don't you know any other tunes?"

"Please," Mr. What said firmly. *"I'm ordering you to find Gustav and bring him to the front door, now."*

The shadow butler's superior sneer fell. "I'll be right back, sir."

He closed the door again.

The Whats half expected another lengthy delay, probably without Gustav at the end of it, but this time the door reopened an instant later.

That instant couldn't have been enough time for the scornful butler to travel down the length of the long hallway, let alone to any of the farther regions of the house, and return with Gustav in tow, but here he was now, escorting Gustav Gloom.

CHAPTER THREE
MR. WHAT HAS EMERGENCY PROCEDURES FOR BEING ATTACKED BY LOBSTERS

The expression on the shadow butler's spotty face was as venomous as a crate filled with snakes.

"The What family," he announced, his every word establishing that he considered this duty beneath him. "Young Master Gloom. Is there anything *else* you would like me to do, sir?"

Gustav didn't seem nearly as out of breath as he should have been after arriving in such a hurry. "Yes."

"I'll keep that in mind," the shadow butler said, just before aiming his nose in the air and striding off with the air of a man whose home has just been sprayed by a skunk.

Mr. What peered after him in dismay. "What's his problem?"

"Him?" Gustav seemed surprised that Mr. What would even bother to ask. "That's just Hives. He's our terrible butler."

Pearlie asked, "Why would you let him work for you if he's such a terrible butler?"

"I think you misunderstand," Gustav said. "He's not a butler who happens to be terrible, but a *terrible butler*."

She gaped. "You mean, being terrible is his job?"

"Yes. He's usually stationed at the door to a room nobody ever uses, so there are never any visitors he can fail to announce, but tonight I ordered him to watch the door in case you came over."

Fernie took Gustav's explanation the same way she took most revelations about the Gloom house: with a sputtering indignation that strained her ability to speak. "Why would you even *want* a terrible butler?"

"My grandpa Lemuel believed that having a terrible butler was better than having a good one. He said that most people with good butlers become boring, because everything is done for them. But people with terrible butlers always have to figure out how to do things for themselves."

"Well, if that's what you want," Fernie reasoned, "wouldn't it make more sense to just not have a butler of any kind?"

"I don't think Grandpa ever thought of that."

Fernie was sputtering again when Mr. What, who'd followed all this with what looked like deep amusement, prodded Gustav: "Gustav, you told the girls you wanted to talk to me about something?"

"Right." Gustav stepped outside and closed the door. For a moment he looked nervous, like an actor suddenly shoved onstage who forgets all his big lines at the first sight of his audience. Then he gulped. "Mr. What, how much did Fernie tell you about what happened to my father and the woman who *would have been* my mother?"

Mr. What's face softened. "She mentioned that something bad happened to them."

Gustav seemed surprised. "Really? She didn't give you any details?"

"No. She didn't say a word."

Gustav shook his head. "I'm a little shocked. Normally she talks so much."

Fernie's jaw dropped wide open.

Pearlie rolled her eyes. "That's what I've been saying all this time. I mean, *hello*?"

Fernie stomped her foot. *"Hey!"*

Mr. What set a protective hand on Fernie's shoulder. "You do talk a lot, dear. But she's also a very smart girl, Gustav. I think she decided that the story belonged to you and wasn't hers to share with us, unless you gave your permission."

Gustav glanced at Fernie, and a brief twitch—not quite a smile, but certainly a look of appreciation—animated the corners of his lips. "Okay. But I don't think I need to get into it now when I can just give her permission to tell you later."

Mr. What nodded warily. "Okay."

"My dad is a prisoner somewhere in the Dark Country. I want to help him, but in order for that to happen, I need you to give Fernie permission to come inside with me."

Mr. What looked as trapped as any good man would be with one child he cared about begging for help that he could only give by risking a child he cared about even more. "Why does it have to be Fernie?"

Gustav was unsurprised by the question. "Because there's somebody inside who knows what I need to know who says that he'll only talk to her."

Mr. What shook his head. "I'm sorry, Gustav, but from what I hear, it's never that simple inside your house. I can't allow it."

"What if you come with us?"

This was something Mr. What hadn't expected. "Excuse me?"

"I'll put you in charge. If anything we do looks too risky, then all you have to do is say so. I'll take you back out and never mention it again. But it should be okay. I've mapped out the dullest route possible and won't take you near anything that should cause us any trouble."

Mr. What looked even more trapped now that somebody had just asked him, in front of the daughters he loved, to prove that he was only a careful man and not an actual coward. "But . . ."

"Mr. What. We're talking about my *father*."

Fernie said, "Please, Dad."

Pearlie added, "You've got to. And take *me* this time. I wanna go."

Mr. What might have refused to get on planes or ride on trains. He might have known what kind of shoes had the most slippery soles and cataloged the most useful emergency procedures for fire, burglary, and being attacked by lobsters. His basement may have been well-stocked with emergency provisions that included flare guns and spray cans of tarantula repellent, and asking him to take a risk on anything was like asking a German shepherd to meow. But he was also a man who had loved his own father, and could not reject the request of a boy who only wanted to know his. He finally said, "Gustav, when I was a boy, we had something we called a pinky swear. It was only used in emergencies, when we needed the absolute truth and nothing but the truth. Do you give me your pinky swear that you won't lead us anywhere dangerous?"

"You have my pinky swear," Gustav said.

The two of them made a big ceremony of linking their little fingers and shaking them, as if this formed the most unbreakable contract ever devised by Man.

Even so, Mr. What could not resist asking one last question. "Are you *sure*?"

"Absolutely sure. I walked the whole route myself, just now, to be sure. I even installed extra safety railings."

Both the What girls burst out laughing.

Sometimes, only the laughter of children can persuade an adult that he's being ridiculous. Mr. What reddened and glanced at his girls, who were struggling mightily to bring their hilarity under control. They almost managed to get themselves together, but then made eye contact with each other and exploded with fresh giggles.

Mr. What tried to look mad, but seemed to have some trouble holding the expression. "Is that true? Did you really go to the trouble of installing extra safety railings, just for my sake?"

"I know you like them," Gustav said earnestly, looking a little startled when the girls started laughing again.

After a moment, Mr. What surprised all three kids by joining in.

"All right, Gustav. As long as you explain where we're going every step of the way, and I get to turn us around the first time I see trouble, then I'll do this for you. Shall we go?"

The girls squealed and wrapped their dad in the tightest of all possible hugs.

The first part of their journey was familiar. It still began with that long walk down the same portrait-lined entrance hall, which again led to the cavernous grand parlor occupied by hundreds of shadowy figures saying things like "Oh, terrific, more party crashers," and "There goes the neighborhood," and in the baffling case of one shadow, tap-dancing across the floor wearing a bow tie wider than his head, "Wakka-bakka-ding-dong-whang-bang-gazoom."

"Don't worry about him," Gustav said. "He does that everywhere."

"Must make him a real hit at parties," Mr. What said.

Mr. What had no problem with Gustav leading them down one of the many side passages, or up a circular stairway, or through a room furnished with hundreds of desks and just as many old-fashioned manual typewriters, clacking away all by themselves even though there was no paper in sight and nobody around to read whatever was being written. (Gustav called that the Hall of All the People Who Liked to Say That They'd Like to Write a Book Someday But Had Never Been Able to Find the Time.)

After one last shortcut through the servant passages that ran behind all the rooms, the corridors they traveled grew dustier and the light dingier in a way that began to strike Fernie as familiar from her last visit. The few shadows wandering these passages alongside Gustav and his friends looked furtive, and even hostile, which led a worried Mr. What to ask Gustav, for the first time since entering the house, whether he was certain that this place was safe.

"It's not pleasant," Gustav admitted. "The shadows in this part of the house aren't as respectable as the ones who hang around in the grand parlor. They can be trouble, but they'll keep their distance tonight. They're all still a little scared of Fernie from the last time."

"The shadows are scared of Fernie?" Pearlie said incredulously.

"Yes. They tried to push her around, and she showed them that it was a big mistake."

"So let that be a lesson to you," Fernie told her older sister.

Pearlie rolled her eyes. "Right. What really happened?"

"I'm not kidding," Gustav insisted. "That's what really happened. Fernie scared them so much that they'll never bother her again. Why don't you believe me?"

"I believe you," said Mr. What with quiet pride.

But then the corridor grew even more dingy and even less respectable, the dark shapes lurking in the corners even less pleasant, until at long last they found themselves standing at their destination, another place Fernie knew: a dead end dominated by a vault door that appeared to have been made from a cross section of some massive tree. The closest thing to a doorknob was a grasping iron hand at its precise center, inviting visitors to clasp it even though its fingernails were long and ragged and sharp enough to cut anybody who tried. Wisps of gray mist puffed through the crack at the bottom of the door.

The sign on the door read:

WARNING
DO NOT ENTER
Hall of Shadow Criminals Within

"Cool," Pearlie breathed.

Mr. What drew back as if stung. "I can't say that I like the looks of this, Gustav."

Fernie knew that she had only a few seconds to reassure her father. "It's okay, Dad. We've been past this door before. It's perfectly safe as long as you watch where you're going and don't stray off the paths."

"What happens if you stray off the paths?"

"Well," Fernie replied, hating to say it but knowing that there was no way out of it, "you fall. There's nothing between them but empty space, so you just go straight down. It's okay as long as you keep an eye on where you're going."

Mr. What looked even more unhappy at this development. "What if you trip over a shoelace or something?"

"We're all wearing loafers," Pearlie pointed out.

"Besides," Gustav said, "I knew you would be concerned, so it's where I installed the safety railings."

Mr. What wasn't mollified. "Let me see."

Gustav grasped the iron hand at the center of the door. As they were designed to, the sharp claws at the ends of the fingers curled inward to scratch his skin, drawing blood from his flesh, before the door rolled aside and revealed the Hall of Shadow Criminals in all its terrible grandeur.

Ahead of them, the white stone paths, arranged like a labyrinth, floated unsupported in a sea of darkness, stretching out as far as the Whats could see. Some of the paths ended in distant stone islands, each one bearing a prisoner in a cell of pure light.

The paths now had safety railings mounted at their edges, protecting travelers from an accidental drop into nothingness. There must have been miles of them. For Fernie, who had walked the same route with Gustav depending only on her own sense of balance, it should have looked much safer, but somehow the railings made the labyrinth look even scarier. Maybe it was because they were reminders that there was still danger here, no matter how hard Gustav tried to protect them from it.

"How?" Fernie managed.

"I ordered Hives to put them up," Gustav said. "I wouldn't rest all my weight on them or anything, because he's Hives and he does only as much work as he has to, but they should be enough to keep you from slipping off the paths by accident. Don't you like them, Mr. What?"

Mr. What's eyes looked glassy. "Please close the door, Gustav. I need to think about this for a few minutes."

Gustav obliged. A quick tug, and the massive door rolled back into place and shut with an echoing *clang*, the iron hand at its center making a brief angry fist before relaxing enough to invite another painful hand clasp.

Mr. What leaned one hand against the wall and gasped, shaking his head in sheer denial of what he had seen.

Pearlie rushed to his side. "You okay, Dad?"

"Fine," he managed. "You know I don't like heights or darkness much, and that place has both. I'll just need a few minutes to get used to the idea."

"That's okay," Gustav said. "I'm grateful to you for coming this far."

Fernie hugged her dad, but found her attention taken by the closed vault door and the memory of the labyrinth beyond. After a moment, she suddenly found herself understanding why they were here, and could only wonder why it had taken her so long; probably because she'd been so busy, all along, worrying about her dad. She exclaimed, "We're here to see Hieronymus Spector!"

CHAPTER FOUR
OF COURSE, SOMETHING GOES TERRIBLY WRONG

Mr. What glanced up at the strange name. "Who's that?"

Fernie answered him. "A nasty shadow criminal we visited on our last trip."

This did not make Mr. What look any happier. "What kind of shadow criminal?"

"The evil kind," Gustav said. "Don't worry, Mr. What—he's in a secure cell by himself and can't do us any harm. But he knows a lot about the Dark Country and shadow history, and has always been the one person I could speak to when I needed information I couldn't get anywhere else."

"Really? What about your great-aunt Mellifluous? Or your friend Mr. Notes? I've met them at our picnics; they're nice. Why can't you ask *them* questions?"

"I could," Gustav said, "if I were asking

them questions about nice things. It gets a little harder if I'm in trouble and have to ask them questions about things that are not so nice."

Mr. What looked more and more upset at himself for agreeing to take his daughters on this dangerous expedition. "And this Hieronymus Spector character? What did he do to get himself put in a cage?"

"That's another long story, Mr. What. It was a terrible crime against both human beings and their shadows. But he'll never be allowed to walk free again."

"And why would he only agree to talk to Fernie?"

"To make things difficult for me, I suppose. Once, when I really needed his help, he refused to talk to me until I brought him one thousand spoons. It took me almost a week to collect them all. Then he said he wouldn't talk to me until I put them back in the same drawers I got them from. It's the only way he has to amuse himself."

"Except," Mr. What presumed, "for whatever horrible thing he did to get put in a cage in the first place."

"That's true," Gustav said. "I think he found that very amusing."

"I'm liking this less and less, Gustav."

"It'll be okay. Honest. All I need Fernie to do is stand outside his cage, well out of his reach, and ask some questions for me. I promise you, he won't be able to get at her, and the whole conversation shouldn't take more than a few minutes."

Mr. What wore the look of a man who had ordered an exotic meal and gotten through half of it only to have someone suddenly explain to him that its name translated to something like "parrot brains with fried lizard eyes." Judging from the number of different facial expressions he made in the length of time it took him to open his mouth, Mr. What changed his mind about a dozen times before deciding.

Then he surprised them all. "All right, Gustav. I'm only doing this because I know how important it is to you. But I'm not letting my daughters go in there, with me or without me, unless I check it out first."

"Dad," Fernie said, "I've already been in there one time before—"

"I *know*, Fernie. But my decision's final. I'll let Gustav take me part of the way in, so I can satisfy myself that it's okay. And I'll only do *that* if he makes sure that there's somebody you can call for help if you run into trouble while we're gone."

Gustav nodded, then reached into his pocket and produced a cylindrical black whistle on a chain. He handed it to Fernie and closed her fingers around it. "Blow this," he said, "if we're not back in ten minutes."

She looked down at the chain. "Gustav, I—"

"Your father's right," Gustav said. "He's only doing for you what I would want my dad to do for me if he were around. Don't worry, it'll be okay. I'm just going to walk your father in for a short distance, prove to him that it's safe, and then walk him back. There should be no problem, but if we're not back in ten minutes or if you run into any other kind of trouble, blow that whistle and somebody I trust with my life will come running to show you the way out."

Fernie hung the chain around her neck. "Okay."

Once again, Gustav clasped the iron hand, which once again tightened to scratch his skin. The great circular door rolled aside, and Gustav crossed the threshold, stepping aside so Mr. What could follow.

Mr. What entered after him, his knees wobbling like they had just been turned to butter. He turned around and faced his girls, hurrying to say something before the door rolled shut behind him. "Remember, girls, be caref—"

The door clanged shut, cutting off the rest.

Pearlie hugged herself. "He was going to say *careful*."

"Thanks," Fernie said with tremendous irritation. "I never would have been able to figure that out without you here to help me."

"Sorry," said Pearlie.

The two girls huddled together at the end of the dingy corridor, a sudden uncomfortable silence wrapping them in its grip as they waited for Gustav and their father to return. Fernie rediscovered something she'd almost forgotten after all the time she'd spent in this house running from one danger or another alongside Gustav: Being in a scary place with a friend who lived there and knew his way around was a lot different from being in that place when the friend was out of sight. Even with her big sister at her side, she felt terribly, terribly lost, the world of light so far away that it might have been the moon.

Pearlie checked her watch. "Five minutes."

It couldn't have been only five minutes, not when it had seemed to be almost twenty. Fernie looked around and found her own shadow hanging on one of the gray walls. The familiar little-girl shape seemed to be trembling, but was that just because Fernie herself was trembling?

Fernie raised her hand and waved it to see what her shadow self would do. It wasn't always the same thing she did, especially not when they were together in the Gloom house. The shadow girl raised her hand, too, and waved it the same way, but a fraction of a second after Fernie did, and with a notable lack of enthusiasm.

Pearlie checked her watch again. "Six minutes."

Fernie shivered and fingered the emergency whistle just to make sure that it still hung from the chain around her neck.

Beside her, Pearlie said, "Something seems wrong."

Fernie almost jumped. "Why? What?"

"I'm not saying it. I'm reading it."

Fernie looked at the door. The legend on the sign had changed. It now read:

WARNING
Hall of Shadow Criminals
SOMETHING SEEMS WRONG

Fernie's heart skipped a beat. "That can't be good."

The sign on the door blurred, the various letters shifting and changing position and finally recombining to form an entirely different legend that read:

WARNING
Hall of Shadow Criminals
THIS IS DOWNRIGHT OMINOUS

Fernie was reduced to arguing with the door. "What? *What?! What's* downright ominous?"

Groping for an innocent explanation, Pearlie said, "Maybe the sign's just making things look worse and worse to keep unauthorized visitors like us from hanging around."

"Maybe," Fernie said, without believing

it. "Or maybe something really *is* downright ominous."

"Maybe we can just open the door and give them a yell. You know, let them know that things are getting pretty scary out here."

The last thing Fernie wanted to do in front of her big sister was agree that things were getting too scary for her to handle. But the air around them was getting colder, and the shadows on the walls were growing darker, and the warning sign was even now blurring a third time. She dreaded seeing what the new words were going to be, but the message remained blurry, the indistinct letters struggling for focus but never quite getting there. It was as if whatever warning they had to impart next was so horrible that they couldn't come up with words that were terrible enough.

Pearlie checked her watch again. "Seven minutes."

The prospect of waiting the full ten was more than Fernie could bear. She jumped to the door and grasped the iron hand, wincing as the sharp clawlike nails on all the fingers scratched her skin. Its tight clasp hurt even more, but the door didn't roll away as it should have, and when she tugged to free her hand, she discovered that it was stuck.

As if realizing that there was now something helpful it could say, the sign came into focus again.

WARNING
Hall of Shadow Criminals
NOW IN EMERGENCY SHUTDOWN
ALL SECURITY PROCEDURES IN EFFECT
DUE TO PRISON BREAK
DO NOT ATTEMPT TO OPEN DOOR
YOU WILL BE HELD IN CUSTODY

Fernie could only yell at the door. "Why didn't you warn me about this before I tried to open you, you stupid *door*!?!" She tried to free her hand, felt a sharp pain, and cried out as the iron hand tightened still further. The claws hadn't made much more than pinprick wounds yet, but they hurt, and the message was clear: If she struggled again, the hand would tighten even more, making the pain that much worse.

Pearlie fell to her knees at Fernie's side. "It's okay. It's okay. Don't panic yet. Gustav gave us that emergency whistle, didn't he? Why don't we blow that?"

Fernie's trapped hand was really beginning to hurt quite a bit now. It was hard to stand perfectly motionless, and the iron hand interpreted even a slight movement on her part as another attempt to escape. "Hurry."

Pearlie took the chain with the whistle from around Fernie's neck, put it around her own, lifted the whistle to her lips, and blew hard. Fernie expected to hear a piercing shriek, something that would summon an army of helpful rescuers from the farthest reaches of the Gloom house, but the only sound that emerged was a sad burp, like their uncle Warren made every time he ate cheese.

Perturbed, Pearlie blew again . . . and this time got an even sadder burp, like the kind Uncle Warren only made when it was *grilled* cheese.

She stared at the whistle as if not recognizing it, and guessed, "Maybe it's like a dog whistle, and it makes a sound that only shadows can hear."

"Maybe," Fernie said. "And maybe it's broken." She glanced at her shadow, who remained silhouetted against the wall, watching her predicament with dark fascination. "Did *you* hear anything when she blew the whistle?"

"Nope," the shadow girl said.

"Neither did I," Pearlie's shadow chimed in, though she hadn't actually been asked.

Pearlie looked mortified. "Sorry. Maybe if we—"

Then the floor started to rumble, not continuously, but off and on, each sudden crash of thunder followed by a moment of uncanny silence. It was the sound the ground makes when something very big and very dangerous draws near, shaking the earth with every step . . . but this monster approached from somewhere inside the house. From where Fernie stood, she could hear glass shattering as paintings fell off walls.

"Something very, very big is coming," Pearlie said, unnecessarily.

The far end of the corridor turned dark as something tremendous lumbered around the bend. It was so big that it had to walk hunched over, its sides scraping the walls and its spine tearing a gouge in the ceiling. It completely filled the space available to it, leaving no possible dodging room for any unlucky creature that might have been trapped in its path. Anything before it was going to be either swallowed whole or trampled beneath its feet.

The good news was that, while the hallway separating the monster from Fernie and Pearlie was distressingly devoid of any doors that might have offered an escape route, there was one last side passage, leading off to the left no more than ten paces away. At the rate the monster was moving, beating it to that only possible escape would not be a problem.

For the trapped Fernie, anything even a step away might as well have been on the other side of the world. But she wasn't the only person here whose life was at stake. "Pearlie! You can still get away! Run!"

Pearlie moved closer. "No."

"There's no reason for you to stay!"

"Yes, there is," Pearlie said. "I call it being your big sister."

The monster was still too far away right now to tell what it looked like—only that it seemed to absorb all the light around it, and that its mouth flashed shiny white fangs as long as Fernie's forearms.

Fernie resisted giving her trapped hand a desperate yank that would have cut it to ribbons. "Pearlie, I'm not kidding here! You've got to go!"

"No," said Pearlie.

Fernie wanted to scream at her for being so stupid, but the next approaching footstep shook the floor so violently that she had to brace herself just to avoid falling. The iron hand interpreted it as an attempt to yank herself free, and punished her in the way that only it could.

Pearlie blew on the emergency whistle three more times, again not succeeding in making any noises more helpful than Uncle Warren's cheese burps. Appalled, she looked at her watch again and said, "Eleven minutes. I don't think Dad and Gustav are coming back."

The monster filling the corridor was now much closer, and almost to the side passage that represented the only possible escape, but it was still impossible to discern its shape, only that it had powerful legs and a tremendous head, and that its teeth were far longer and sharper than Fernie wanted to think about.

She didn't believe it would have any trouble at all swallowing her and Pearlie in a single gulp.

CHAPTER FIVE
THE ONE THING SMART PEOPLE DO WHEN THEY'RE BEING CHASED BY MONSTERS

All of a sudden, the iron hand loosened, and Fernie's hand slid free, marked with ugly red scratches a lot like the ones she'd suffered when Harrington had been playing with her favorite pen and she'd been a little too insistent about trying to get it back.

She stumbled a step away from the door, not knowing what had happened, wanting to run from the approaching monster while there was still a chance, but not wanting to leave her father and best friend behind in the Hall of Shadow Criminals. She might have remained frozen with indecision until the approaching monster was upon them, but then the door rolled aside and the familiar voice of Gustav Gloom cried, "Girls! Do what I say and run!"

Fernie was so close to bolting out of sheer panic anyway that she didn't think of turning around to confirm that her father was with him. She just ran, a step behind Pearlie, who ducked into the side corridor to their left and began to pick up speed.

Just before she ducked into the same side passage herself, Fernie glanced up at the approaching monster, which was almost upon the intersection. Like so many of the shadows of the Gloom house, it looked like a real thing now that she had a chance to see it close up, allowing her to see more details than just its general outline. She saw that its skin was scaled, that its eyes were dark blots recessed beneath bony, overhanging brows, that its mouth was wide, and that despite its attempts to hunch over as it forced its way through a corridor much too small for it, its spine still scraped along the ceiling, carving a deep furrow with every step it took. The teeth looked longer and more worth avoiding than ever.

It was only after she made it into the side passage, arms pumping as she raced after the fleeing form of her sister, that Fernie realized it was a shape she knew.

It was, impossible as it was for her to believe, the shadow of a Tyrannosaurus rex.

Fernie already knew that there were shadow dinosaurs in Gustav's house. She hadn't actually seen one before now, but had heard them during her hurried visit to the dinosaur bedroom.

Seeing one close up, feeling its meaty breath on her skin, and hearing it bellow in frustration as she scurried away down the side passage a step before it would have eaten her were just the kinds of things Gustav had so recently promised her father they'd be avoiding this trip.

"Gustaaaaaaav!" she yelled. "You'd better have a good explanation for this!"

Gustav yelled back, "Can it *wait*?"

The corridor resounded with a horrible crash. Fernie risked stopping long enough to turn around, and after a fleeting glimpse of Gustav racing by her, saw the cause. This side corridor where they had retreated was narrower than the one they had left, and had a much lower ceiling. The tyrannosaur, who had already been walking with its head down, now had to force its gigantic frame into an even smaller space.

It had trouble changing direction wherever there wasn't enough room to turn, and the intersection between the wider passage and this narrower, smaller passage was a cramped space indeed. The tyrannosaur poked its massive head into the smaller space, advanced, encountered a wall, backed up, entered the narrow corridor at another angle, got a little farther in before encountering a wall, and backed up again.

The main problem seemed to be the tyrannosaur's giant tail. It could only bend so much, and it stuck out so far behind the monster's legs that it kept slamming into the wall of the other corridor and made getting any farther into this one too clumsy to manage in one try. The tyrannosaur could only advance by degrees, moving forward and backing up and moving forward and backing up, each time turning a little more so it could eventually face the right way to head down the passage where Fernie stood.

Something about the creature's presence here, at this moment, didn't make sense to her, even in a house where so much didn't make sense to her. In this house, there was something that didn't make any sense every ten feet. But Fernie had the idea she was missing something, something important. She found herself staring at the advancing monster, tilting her head first one way and then the other, as if changing the angle of what she saw would suddenly make it right.

The tyrannosaur grew impatient and used its giant head like a battering ram, making craters of the walls near the junction and tearing itself an easier entrance to the side corridor. Part of the ceiling collapsed down around its head, raising clouds of dust. Its great nostrils flared, clouds billowed, and the tyrannosaur forced itself farther into the side passage, ripping a giant bite from another section of ceiling and crunching it to pieces in its jaws just so there'd be more room for its SUV-size head.

Somewhere far behind her, Pearlie screamed at her to run. Gustav yelled that if she didn't wake up, she was going to die. Fernie didn't hear her father's voice also calling for her, and that seemed wrong, too: the kind of wrong that was terribly, terribly important but couldn't fit in her head any more than the tyrannosaur could.

"Dad!" she cried. "Where are you?"

The tyrannosaur bellowed as loudly as an entire herd of elephants and forced itself ten feet closer to her, its head ripping a deeper furrow in the ceiling while its broad shoulders tore gouges in the walls on both sides. It was almost upon her now, its comically small arms clutching at air. It was so close that Fernie could have taken two steps toward it, reached up with one arm, and tapped it on the chin—though that certainly didn't seem like a good idea for a girl whose immediate plans did not include becoming somebody else's lunch.

The cavernous nostrils snuffed, expelling a cloud of mist that drenched her.

The thing roared again, and then, impossibly, *spoke*.

"I'm coming to *get* you, Fernie What . . ."

All of Fernie's paralysis vanished in an instant.

She let out an *eek*.

She was not proud of *eek*ing, but she *eek*ed, anyway.

She threw up her hands and *eek*ed and ran away as fast as she could, aware from the sounds of destruction behind her that the tyrannosaur who'd just called her by name was willing to tear down all the walls in the house to reach her.

She ran and headed toward the dim place where the passage turned to the right not far ahead. Pearlie and Gustav were both there, yelling at her that she wasn't moving quickly enough. The sounds of destruction pursued her, little pieces of debris peppered her legs, and still she ran, screaming, wondering why her father wasn't up there with Pearlie and Gustav.

It all seemed to be part of the same puzzle, but she didn't have time to think about it, not with that terrible dinosaur *coming to get her*. She was still wondering what had gone wrong, still trying to put the clues together in her head, when a furious Pearlie, seizing her by the wrist, yanked her around the bend.

Her older sister fumed. "What's the *matter* with you, anyway? You see a monster like that coming after you, and you don't have anything better to do than to stand there *staring* at it?"

The corridor up ahead stretched as far as Fernie's eyes could see, every step of it lined with doors: tiny mouse-size doors, cat flaps, giant stone gates, glass office doors with transoms, doors shaped like cartoon lightning bolts, and doors that looked like somebody without much artistic talent had taken a dull crayon and drawn a door with his eyes closed. Gustav stood beside one open door, out of which streamed a flickering orange light. Despite that, he looked paler, thinner, and somehow grayer than usual, as if whatever happened to him and Mr. What in the Hall of Shadow Criminals had robbed him of the usual sharp contrast between his pale skin and black suit.

Mr. What was nowhere in sight.

Fernie stumbled over her words. "The dinosaur . . ."

"I *saw* it," Pearlie said. "I didn't stop and turn around so I could get a good look, but I did see it. That's why I was *running*. Smart people *run* when they're being chased by monsters. *Stupid* people don't."

Fernie couldn't help resenting being spoken to that way, because in the few weeks they'd all been living across the street from the Gloom house, she was the member of the family who'd spent the most time here, and she didn't need her big sister to tell her that running from monsters was a good thing. As far as Fernie was concerned, she had more than enough personal experience with that activity.

It was just that *this* time, there was something . . .

The crashing and tearing sounds resumed behind her, cutting off the thought before she could finish it. "Where's Dad?"

"He's okay," Gustav said, making Fernie feel about a million times better in the span of two words.

"But why isn't he *here*?"

"I'll tell you in a little bit," said Gustav.

"That's not good enough, Gustav! Where's—"

Another savage roar and another cacophony of crashing noises behind them established why Gustav might not have been willing to indulge in a long complicated explanation right now. A cloud of dust and debris, wafted aloft by tyrannosaur breath, turned the air gritty around them, making Fernie cough; it was not the first time she'd coughed in a house that in some places could have welcomed a battalion of maids bearing an entire armory of feather dusters.

"He's going to keep coming," Gustav said, "until he loses our scent. We have to move quickly. Don't ask any questions. Just follow me and don't stop until I say it's okay to stop. Okay?"

The girls both gave their okays.

Gustav ducked through the open door that radiated the orange light. The girls ran after him and down the long circular stone stairway on the other side. The wedge-shaped steps, narrowing to points at the center of the circle, were moist and dotted with slippery patches of moss; there were no railings to hold on to, and the orange light from the torches burning on the wall flickered so much that it was hard to see where the steps were. Still, Gustav moved with the speed that only a boy raised by creatures as fleeting as shadows could, and the girls had to take the treacherous steps two or three at a time just to stay in sight of the dark little shape forever disappearing around the bend.

They were about half a dozen turns down by the time Fernie noticed that the lit torches grew fewer and farther apart the farther down they went, and that as a result, the stairwell was getting darker.

The stairs were by now so much a direct violation of every rule their father had about staircases—they had to be well lit, they had to have railings, they needed to be dry, and they should never be taken at a headlong run—that the girls stopped on their own, even though they both had enough wind left to run much farther.

Fernie called, "Gustav?"

He was somewhere just ahead of them, out of sight. "What?"

"Where are we going?"

"To catch up with your dad."

"Why isn't he with you?"

A pale sliver of Gustav's face, the only part of him visible past the sharp line where a deeper darkness began, appeared from around the next bend.

"I'm sorry," Gustav said. "We got separated. But he's okay, I promise you."

Fernie didn't know why, since she'd never had any reason to doubt Gustav before, but she found herself not believing him.

Pearlie spoke her worry aloud. "He's not okay, Gustav."

The one visible side of Gustav's face formed a frown. "Why would I lie to you about something like that?"

"I don't think you're lying," Pearlie told him. "But I don't think you know our dad the way we do. He worries about us all the time. He checks on us if we're making noise, and he checks on us if we're being too quiet. If some kind of emergency's come up and he can't get to us right away, he's not okay. He's *not* okay. Wherever he is, I promise you, he's going crazy with worry."

Gustav licked his lips and peered over their heads. "The tyrannosaur—"

Pearlie put her hands on her hips. "I don't hear it coming anymore. Fernie, do *you* still hear it coming?"

Fernie realized that she hadn't heard either the damage the monster made or its unnerving promises to come get her since entering the stairwell.

"So all we know," Pearlie continued, anger building in every word, "is that there was some kind of prison break and that you got separated from our dad somehow, after promising him that none of us would be in any danger."

Gustav glanced at Fernie, as if hoping she'd talk some sense into her older sister. "But I'm taking you to where he's going to *be* . . ."

The sudden whininess in his voice, so different from the way he usually sounded, was enough to persuade Fernie that she really needed to demand an explanation right now. She folded her arms over her chest and said, "Pearlie's right. I think you need to tell us what's going on."

Gustav didn't move for several seconds. Then he sighed in defeat and climbed the several steps separating him from them. Even as he moved into the direct light of the nearest burning torch, the sense Fernie had gotten before, that he was even paler and more colorless than usual, grew sharper and harder to deny.

Then Fernie realized that she could see the flickering of the torchlight on the moist walls, not just behind him but *through* him.

"Touch me," he said.

Fernie reached for his cheek.

Her fingers passed right through him. It was as if he wasn't even there—though he was as much *there* as the beings with whom Gustav Gloom had spent all of his short and unquiet life.

Fernie exhaled, thinking she understood. "You're not Gustav. You're Gustav's *shadow*."

This wouldn't have been so bad if it were true, since Gustav's shadow had been, on at least one other occasion, as helpful as Gustav himself.

But then he shook his head, with a sadness great even for a boy who had known so much of that feeling in his life. "No, Fernie. I'm Gustav, all right. I've just been *turned into* a shadow."

CHAPTER SIX
GUSTAV IS A SHADOW OF HIS FORMER SELF

The two girls both exploded with a flurry of questions, both of them speaking over the other and burying most of what either of them said behind a jumble of desperate babble.

Fernie cried, "How did you get turned into a shadow? And where's my dad? What's with that dinosaur? Who escaped from the prison? Why didn't your emergency whistle work? What's gone wrong?"

But even as she said that, Pearlie cried over her, "What happened to Dad? And what do you mean, you got turned into a shadow? Why are we being chased by a dinosaur? Why didn't your whistle work? What's gone wrong? Is our dad going to be okay?"

They glanced at each other, not just aggravated and terrified, but suddenly mortified into silence.

Gustav held up both hands to halt the barrage of questions. "I don't know why that dinosaur's running around loose or what it wants with us. I don't know why the emergency whistle didn't work; maybe it got broken somehow while I wasn't looking. I don't know exactly how many prisoners escaped. Your dad and I had to rush ourselves to safety when the prison break began and didn't have time to keep track. I don't know where your dad is now, but I do know where he's heading, and I'm pretty sure he'll be safe until we get there."

This was the kind of answer Fernie had heard too many times from Gustav Gloom. "You haven't explained how you turned into a shadow."

Gustav shrugged. "I'm not sure about that, either, but I have some ideas. Can I go into more detail on the way?"

Fernie and Pearlie glanced at each other, had an entire conversation of the sort certain sisters can have without ever saying a word, and made a silent decision.

Fernie said, "We'll follow you. But I need to take a look at my hurt hand first."

"Okay," said Gustav.

Fernie had been so busy running for her life and then asking unanswered questions that the cuts on her hand had forgotten to hurt. Now that she looked at it, the throbbing started anew. There were red scratches on the back of her hand, extending up her wrists; none of them were bleeding badly, and none of them were deeper than past ones Harrington had given her while still a playful kitten yet to know the sharpness of his own claws, but they were still ugly, and they still hurt.

Pearlie asked a stupid question. "Does it hurt?"

Fernie gave her an irritated look. "Yes."

The scratches would likely hurt a lot more when she found her way back to some disinfectant. Right now, she would have given her favorite zombie-head coin bank at home for some bandages just to keep them clean.

"All right," she said. "Let's go."

They followed Gustav farther down the spiral staircase, descending into deep darkness as the torches lining the walls grew even fewer and farther between. It was no longer possible to run in these conditions, especially with the steps and the walls growing more moist with every second, the little light there making the stone glisten with beads of cold light.

Gustav said, "First off, your dad's being led to the room I call the Hall of Almost Happiness. I promise you, it's one of the house's safest places."

Fernie was too concerned with other questions to ask for a description. "Who's taking him there?"

"My shadow. When everything started going bad in the Hall of Shadow Criminals, I asked him to lead your dad out the back way while I went out the front entrance and collected you. That tyrannosaur complicates things, and we might have to take some strange detours, but I don't think we'll have any problems."

"If you're a shadow now," Pearlie pointed out, "and your shadow's out there somewhere helping our dad, then that makes you a shadow with a shadow."

"Yes. So?"

"So that doesn't make sense."

"Sure it does. Do you ever find yourself walking in a place where light's coming from more than one source? Did you ever look down and see more than one shadow of yourself, one lighter than the other? That's your shadow and your shadow's shadow. My shadow's been around a long time, and it isn't about to disappear just because I've become a shadow myself. It just means that we'll be more evenly matched when we have our thumb-wrestling contests."

Fernie slipped on a patch of moss and steadied herself with a palm against the wall. Her injured hand was immediately drenched. The water dripping down the walls had become a torrent, pouring down the stones in waves. More had collected on the steps and continued to pour downward, turning the stairs into a shallow cascade.

"It's getting deep," she noted.

"It'll get much deeper," Gustav assured her. "All part of the plan."

They passed another torch. This one could barely stay lit, the water was dripping on it so hard. It was now almost impossible to discern the shadow Gustav had become from all the darkness surrounding him, but that seemed a small matter next to finding safe places to step.

Ahead of them, he said, "What next? Oh, yes: How I became a shadow. I don't think I got to that part yet."

"I don't think you've satisfied us with any of the other parts, either," Pearlie muttered.

He grunted. "I was always told that I *might* become a shadow someday, but never really thought that I *would*."

Pearlie asked him, "Why would you even think it *could* happen?"

"One of the things my shadow mother taught me, before she disappeared, was that a half child, half shadow like me is a very rare thing that's only existed a handful of other times in the entire history of the world. She said that in most cases, kids like me live as halfsies, part one thing and part the other, until some sudden fright pushes them off the fence one way or the other, and they become either all child or all shadow. I guess all the excitement in the Hall of Shadow Criminals must have been enough to do the trick. I'm a shadow for good now."

There was a difference between how calmly he said it and how much Fernie knew his heart must have been breaking. She said, "Didn't you always tell me that you wanted to be like other kids, living on the other side of the fence?"

Gustav seemed a little surprised at the question. "Did I say that? I don't remember."

This, too, seemed wrong to Fernie, just another of the many things that had happened since the prison break that didn't fit together. She was about to ask a skeptical question when she descended another step into darkness and found herself suddenly knee-deep in cold water.

This surprised her so much that she stumbled off the riser and, yelling, belly flopped into the flood that had completely submerged the lower sections of stairs. She hadn't expected to go swimming today and wouldn't have done it in the dark, with her clothes on; certainly not at the bottom of a set of circular stairs. She went under the surface for a second, screamed a stream of bubbles, then thrashed her way to the surface in time to see her older sister's head pop up just a couple of feet away.

Gustav stood with his shoes on the surface of the water, peering down at them. "Are you okay?"

Fernie sputtered. "No, we're not okay! Why is there water at the bottom of your *staircase*?!?"

"It's not a staircase," he said. "Well, it might have been once, before the walls sprouted all those leaks up above, but right now it's really a well with steps. It started filling up long ago, and four of the five lowest levels are all underwater.

Didn't I mention that?"

Pearlie, who'd managed to set her feet on one of the submerged steps and now stood in water up to her shoulders, coughed out water and said, "I thought you promised our dad you'd point out any possible dangers along the way."

"This isn't really a danger," Gustav said. "It's a bit cold, but it's still only water. Swimming down's still the fastest route to where I sent your dad."

Fernie found a step to stand on and wiped the cold water from her eyes. "How can it possibly be the fastest route?"

"Well, let me rephrase it. It's the fastest route that'll keep that crazy dinosaur from following us. You ever see one of those old movies where somebody on the run from people hunting him with dogs crosses a stream to throw the hunters off the scent? Once the two of you pass through water, that tyrannosaur will lose the trail."

Pearlie shivered. "Anybody ever tell you that your house is stupid?"

"I think it's been said once or twice. Come on, it's only a short swim."

The sense that something here didn't add up was now a constant buzz in Fernie's head that she couldn't put out no matter how hard she tried. It was like the feeling she got when she was lying in bed early in the morning, deep in that state exactly halfway between being awake and being asleep, and couldn't quite understand what the buzzing sound from her alarm clock meant. She knew that it seemed urgent but was not able to figure out why.

Next to her, Pearlie said, "You'll show us the way, right?"

"Of course," Gustav said. "The only thing is, it's best if we go one at a time. You follow me first, and I'll come back right away for Fernie." He sank into the water without making a ripple, not stopping until he was only half a shadowy boy's head, just above the surface. It didn't affect his voice at all as he said, "Ready?"

"In a minute," Pearlie said. She took three deep breaths, each heavier and hungrier than the last, and then dove in, just a second before Fernie—still trying to figure out the reason for that inner alarm—would have shouted *NO!*

The water splashed against the stones, churning hard as Pearlie disappeared; and then it started to smooth out, becoming just a black mirror, as hard to see through as spilled ink.

Fernie was alone.

CHAPTER SEVEN
DOWNSTAIRS, UNDERWATER, AND AFTERWARD

For the last several minutes, she hadn't liked Gustav one bit.

That was what Fernie had realized too late, that had made her want to shout *No*.

That was odd. Normally she liked Gustav a lot. She'd liked him from the very first words he'd spoken to her from the other side of his iron fence. She'd liked him even as he'd proven aggravating in a thousand different ways and irritating in a thousand more. She'd liked him even as she'd shared adventures with him in a house that was so much a part of him that it was almost impossible to imagine him living anywhere else.

Sometimes people meet friends who are just so perfect as friends that they instantly fit together like two puzzle pieces that were always meant to come together. She had come to think of Gustav as one of those friends. She felt safe around him, even when the two of them were doing insanely dangerous things.

But since before entering the circular stairway, Fernie hadn't felt safe around Gustav at all.

The Gustav she knew would have given her more answers without being pushed. He would have warned her about the water at the bottom of the stairs before she fell in. He would have been sadder about becoming all shadow when he wanted to be all boy. He would have been more apologetic about the emergency whistle not working, and about getting her whole family into danger when he'd so earnestly promised not to.

He had changed since becoming all shadow, and not in any way she liked.

Fernie looked at the black water on all sides and couldn't escape the sudden certainty that if she stayed here and waited for Gustav to return, her father and sister were lost.

So she took three deep breaths and dove in herself.

The water had the terrible slimy feel that some lake water has, which was one key reason, aside from her father's worries about submerged tree trunks, that she preferred to do her swimming in pools and oceans instead of in ugly, icky, nasty lakes. There was no way to see where she was going, but the stairs did curve downward around that center wall, and she could keep heading down by pulling herself along the stones. The water was so cold that it gave her the same kind of headache that always made her hold her head in her hands after she ate ice cream too fast. She almost wished that she could turn into a shadow herself, just so she could make the swim less unpleasant, but then realized it wasn't the kind of thing a girl should wish for, and just concentrated on pulling herself down along the stairs.

When she'd descended twenty steps, the water pressure started to hurt the top of her head. By the time she'd pulled herself only a few feet farther, she wanted to take a breath so badly, it was like somebody had set a fire inside her ribs.

She knew that if she swam down much farther, there would not be any point in turning back, because there was already barely enough air in her to fuel her return to the surface. But her family was in front of her, and there was nothing but darkness and a cold, dark wait behind her, so she pulled herself farther down, hoping to see some sign of light around the next bend.

Instead, something that felt like a strand of spiderweb brushed across her face.

Bubbles exploded from her mouth as she clutched at her face to sweep the nasty thing away. One touch and she felt a chill deeper than the temperature of the water. Her hands closed around it, snatching it from the current that had left it tumbling through the water.

It was the necklace with the useless emergency whistle. The last time she'd seen it had been around Pearlie's neck.

She screamed, releasing the last of her air in a stream of bubbles. She spun and kicked hard, no longer sure that she was headed in the right direction and no longer sure that it mattered.

She found herself up against the jagged stone ceiling, banging on it as if her strength alone could possibly be enough to make it break and let her pass.

She closed her eyes, sure that this was what drowning felt like.

It was, actually, but drowning usually doesn't end with opening your eyes a little while later and finding yourself not just alive and unhurt but completely dry.

"I told you to wait for me," Gustav Gloom complained.

He sat beside her on the curling stone steps of what seemed to be the very same flooded staircase she'd just been drowning in, except that these steps were dry, well lit by enough torches to do the job, and completely unencumbered by either running water or patches of moss.

He was still a shadow, of course; Fernie could see through him, where the flames of one of the wall torches were dancing. They shone brightest through his eyes, making them look red.

Pearlie was nowhere to be seen.

Fernie asked, "How . . . ?"

He pointed upward. "Look."

She did, and saw one of the most remarkable sights she'd ever encountered in the Gloom house. The air immediately above her head was a smooth black surface, moving to and fro in smooth, lazy ripples. The stairs ascended into it and disappeared.

She raised a trembling hand to this strange

liquid ceiling and found that her fingers went right through, just as they would have if she'd poked them into the surface of a pond. She recognized the feeling of cold water against her skin and pulled her hand back into the bubble of dry air where she and Gustav sat. Her fingers were dry again.

The water didn't seem willing to descend any farther into the stairwell than where she sat, not even by allowing the hand that had invaded it to remain wet.

She stuck her arm back into the water and swished it all about, making bubbles rise, then pulled it back to where she was, and again found that her skin remained dry, not retaining even a single drop.

She looked at Gustav.

He said, "I *told* you that four of the five lowest levels were flooded. The lowest level, where we are, is the dry one. It has to be in order for anybody to use the door at the bottom of the stairs."

She came within a hair's breadth of telling him, for perhaps the millionth time, that his house was stupid. She only stopped herself because something in his impatient expression warned her that it would not be the greatest of ideas. Instead, she said, "I was drowning . . ."

"That's right. That's because you didn't follow my directions and wait for me."

Gustav said this far more coldly than he'd ever spoken to her before. She was struck again by the sense that something must have been terribly wrong for a boy who had been so patient with her for so long to suddenly show such flashes of anger.

She said, "Did you rescue me?"

"No. I didn't come back in time to rescue you. But I didn't have to. As soon as you passed out, you started to sink, and once that happened, you just tumbled down the stairs until you popped back into open air again. You were lucky that you didn't come to a complete stop with your head still in water. I could have found you lying here with everything under your neck in dry air and everything above it nice and drowned in water."

She shuddered. "I don't even feel like I've been coughing."

"In case you haven't figured it out," he said, in a way that called her a stupid girl without actually using those words, "that's the way it works here. You didn't bring any of the water with you, not even the part you'd already swallowed or inhaled."

She sat up straight, felt the very top of her head brush water, and let it stay there, because she found its cooling touch helped her stay calm while talking to this new, different, and not very nice Gustav. "What about Pearlie?"

"What *about* her?"

"Is she okay?"

He seemed to take this as a personal affront. "Why wouldn't she be okay?"

"Gustav! Please! I know that you're mad at me, but tell me that my sister is okay!"

He blinked several times, as if showing concern for a sister was the kind of thing that never would have occurred to him. "Yes, she's okay."

"Where is she? Is she with my dad?"

He needed a couple of seconds to work that out. "No. Your dad's still a little bit farther ahead. Pearlie's just been through a lot and needed to sit down a bit, so I left her in a safe room, just up ahead, and told her to stay there while I came back for you. We should hurry, or she'll get worried."

Fernie nodded, pretending that this made sense to her, but inside was even more certain something had gone horribly wrong and that Gustav was lying. Pearlie was, after all, the girl who had stayed by her side even when the tyrannosaur was coming and staying meant probably giving up the chance to save herself. Agreeing to sit around on her butt somewhere while Gustav went back for Fernie was just not the kind of thing Pearlie would have done, or the kind of thing anybody who knew Pearlie for even five minutes would have thought she could have done.

But why was Gustav lying?

Why was Fernie suddenly so sure that telling him she knew he was lying would be a very bad idea?

She couldn't keep the quaver out of her voice. "Okay. Let's go."

He turned his back on her and for just a moment glanced away, down the remaining curve of the steps.

He was still looking away when she pulled herself down a couple of steps so she could stand up without poking her head into the water. Something shifted under her left leg, and groping to see what it was, she discovered it to be the chain of the necklace with the useless emergency whistle.

She'd been lying on it, and therefore, without meaning to, hiding it with her body.

As useless as it had proven to be, it suddenly seemed like a bad idea to let Gustav know she had it.

So she scooped up both the whistle and the chain in her right hand, wrapping them up in a tight fist just before Gustav turned around to see how she was doing.

He scowled. "Haven't you gotten up yet?"

She rose, wobbling unsteadily on her feet. "I did just come close to drowning, you know."

"That wasn't my fault," he muttered.

She stood, swayed a little bit as if dizzy, and turned away from him, as if needing to test her balance. In fact, her balance was just fine. She'd recovered from her ordeal in the water, was neither unsteady nor dizzy, and wobbled only because she wanted to. She just needed to hide what her right hand was doing as she slipped the emergency whistle and its chain into the pocket of her jeans.

It was terrible to believe that she no longer

trusted the boy who had so quickly become the best friend she'd ever had, or that she needed to keep secrets from him. But the feeling would not go away, and it couldn't be just because he'd become a shadow.

She turned back to him just in time to see him try to hide the terrible darkness in the expression he'd worn while she wasn't looking.

It was the expression of a boy who hated her.

She pretended she hadn't noticed it. "All right. Let's go."

He said, "Okay. Stay close. There might still be escaped shadow criminals about."

He floated ahead, leading her down the final curve of the circular staircase, which ended in a wooden door adorned with the stenciled legend: CORRIDOR 23,973 (SECTION 7(B), NORTHWEST EXTENSION). He opened the door, revealing another of the house's endless corridors, this one much taller and wider than the one that had proven so difficult for the tyrannosaur. It was a fancier corridor, too, probably a "better neighborhood," as Gustav would have put it, marked with a brilliant red carpet runner extending to the left and right until it disappeared into the distance on both sides.

With the single exception of one room Fernie had been to on her last visit that came equipped with its own sun, the corridor was also the best-lit place Fernie had ever seen in the Gloom house, as the ceiling was lined with ornate golden chandeliers, all of which sported dozens of burning candles, casting the walls and all the paintings that lined the vast distance with a burnished orange glow.

"She's this way," said Gustav, turning left.

Fernie had become so uncomfortable around Gustav that she had to resist the temptation to run for her life in the opposite direction. "Okay."

They walked, a floating Gustav leading the way and Fernie walking behind him. The paintings on the walls, all of empty suits without any obvious people in them, offered no clue about how safe the way might be. The doors between the paintings were all hard dark oak, with massive brass knockers hanging from each. There were peepholes above the knockers, some of which darkened for a second or two as Gustav and Fernie passed, indicating that beings behind those doors watched but preferred to stay in hiding.

They walked farther than it made sense for

Gustav to have gone if he had just left Pearlie somewhere safe and returned for Fernie. But then they stopped at a plain wooden door, one of the few without a peephole or a giant brass knocker, and he said, "Here. We'll just pick up Pearlie and then go get your dad."

The door swung inward at his touch. He stepped back and gallantly stepped aside so she could enter first.

Fernie hesitated at the doorway, because the room was darker than the corridor outside and her eyes needed a second or two to adjust. She saw a book-lined study, corners shrouded in impenetrable blackness, and her sister, Pearlie, sitting in an easy chair far too large for her. She was not quite facing the door, because her head was slumped and her hair had fallen forward, making a curtain over her eyes.

The dangling hair offered enough gaps to reveal her cheeks were wet in a way that looked like she'd been crying. That was scary enough all by itself, because Pearlie, like Fernie, didn't cry all that often and pretty much indulged herself in that activity only when things were hopeless. She hadn't even cried the day she'd broken her wrist falling off the swing, and that had happened way back when she was eight. But her shoulders shook now, the way shoulders do when the person they belong to has cried enough to gasp for breath.

The oddest element, and therefore the most frightening, was the red balloon tied to the armrest. Fernie didn't like the way it bobbed about all by itself, almost as if there was something inside it, moving it about in ways that the still air did not.

Fernie took a single step toward her sister and then stopped, realizing that the darkness in the room was not just darkness, but shadow: shadow that swirled around the lonely easy chair and the girl in it like a great black blanket being whipped about with angry hands.

She heard a whispered *shhhh* from that darkness, clearly not meant for her ears.

"What are you waiting for?" asked Gustav, not a single trace of trustworthiness left in a voice that no longer sounded like the boy she knew. *"Go in."*

Fernie wanted nothing more than to rush to her sister's side. But she also knew, as surely as she knew that the sky is up and the ground is down, that if she were foolish enough to cross that threshold, nobody in the world would ever see her, or her sister, or their father, ever again.

The shadow beside her raged: *"Do what I say, you stupid child! Go in!"*

There was no place to flee, no help Fernie could ask for; just the certainty that if she didn't do something desperate, right now, all was lost.

The only thing she could do was call for help, in a manner that had already failed to work once.

She put the whistle to her lips and blew for her life.

CHAPTER EIGHT
THE USEFULNESS OF DOOR KNOCKERS

The emergency whistle made exactly the same useless burping sound it had made before.

The creature who had clearly only been pretending to be Gustav snarled, in a voice like a heavy stone dragged across broken glass, *"You loathsome brat! How dare you?"*

He didn't look much like Gustav anymore; his face had distorted, one side melting like candle wax while the other side blew up like a balloon on the verge of bursting. His teeth had elongated and turned pointy, like fangs. For a heartbeat he throbbed, and he seemed about to become the shadow of a wan, desperately friendly, pigtailed little girl.

The waif looked familiar, but Fernie didn't have time to think about where she'd seen her before, not with the creature grabbing for her with arms grown as elongated as pythons.

Fernie yelled and threw herself to the floor, scrambling away on her back as the shadow arms, which no longer had hands at the ends of them but vicious, snarling snake heads, swung downward to clutch for her.

There was a whoosh of movement, and the angry shadow bellowed in incoherent rage as Fernie's own shadow leaped off the floor and hurled herself on top of him.

Fernie's shadow cried out, *"Fernie! Run! I won't be able to hold him for long!"*

Fernie didn't react right away, because she was too busy remembering exactly where she'd seen the shadow waif's face before.

On her last visit to the Hall of Shadow Criminals, the dangerous creature who had just posed as Gustav had worn the shape of an innocent, heartbroken little girl, locked in one of the cells by mistake. In a voice as sweet as honey, she'd begged for Fernie to free her.

On that night, which had been *almost* as terrible as this one, Fernie had *almost* been fooled by her pathetic offers of devotion, *almost* been cajoled into facing the no doubt disastrous consequences that would have resulted from setting her free.

Fernie hadn't given much thought to the

encounter afterward, because there had been a greater threat to deal with on that night and not much reason to worry about threats from a monster who seemed safely caged—but she did remember being told, later on, that his name had been Nebuchadnezzar.

Now, Nebuchadnezzar changed shapes faster than her eyes could keep up, turning the little-girl head into the features of a ravenous tiger, the tiger into a whirling ball of knives, and the ball of knives into something that no language on earth had ever described and no language on earth ever would.

Fernie's shadow fought him with the same kind of ferocity she always used in defending her human, peppering the many changing heads with as many punches and kicks as she could. "Go! I said *go*!"

Fernie was paralyzed by her concern for Pearlie. She glanced through the open doorway, saw her slumped sister in the easy chair, and wondered if she had time to run in and rescue her while Nebuchadnezzar was occupied. It would only take a second . . .

But then Nebuchadnezzar bellowed, "Carlin! Ursula! Otis! *Get the stupid girl!*"

The shadows wrapping Pearlie in darkness slid away from her slumped form and began to roll toward the door.

Fernie's shadow screamed, "I said *run!*"

Fernie had no choice. She turned tail and fled down the long carpeted hallway, the only thought in her head a prayer that she'd be able to come back and save her sister from these fiends later.

She heard the voices of her pursuers close behind her: three different voices, each one hateful in its own way.

The first was the voice of an arrogant older man, filled with the gravel that only enters a human voice during a bad cold or after twenty years of smoking cigars. "Oh, please. She can't really believe she has a chance."

The second voice belonged to a younger woman and was both cruel and joyous, the kind of voice only heard from somebody who delights in being bad. "I can't say I blame her, Carlin! I'd run, too, if I faced the fate she does! Wouldn't you, Otis?"

The third voice reeked of stupidity. It wasn't the stupidity of someone who simply wasn't smart and therefore had no choice about whether he was being smart or not, but the stupidity of someone who had discovered that being a bully in the service of other bullies was much easier than ever stopping to think about what he was doing. "I dunno, Ursula. I just like it when they run."

They were shadows that moved with the speed of all shadows and had no trouble keeping up with a ten-year-old girl, even if that girl happened to be brilliant at running. So they had a little fun with her, flying alongside her and laughing at her vain attempts to gain ground.

Of the two to Fernie's left, one—probably Carlin—was a gangly old gentleman wearing a three-piece suit and a derby, his hollow cheeks curling back to reveal an oversized smile filled with many needle-shaped teeth. It was the kind of determined smile a rude person gives when he's pretending to be nice but still wants you to know that he thinks you smell bad.

The other, Ursula, possessed the dark, icy-cold, not very enviable kind of beauty that some very attractive young women achieve only when they take deep pleasure in also being terrible people. Her gray-white, ankle-length hair billowed around her like a cloud, in places hard to distinguish from her long white gown. Her full lips drew back, forming a dazzling smile as she saw the depth of Fernie's fear.

With those two to Fernie's left, the one called Otis had to be to her right, so she risked a quick look—and just as quickly wished she hadn't. Otis was a shadow of a repugnant little man with fat cheeks, a squashed nose, and tiny little eyes. Considering his striped shirt, mismatched suspenders, and oversized shoes, he might have been the shadow of a circus clown, but there was nothing at all funny about the leer that had as many missing spaces as misshapen teeth. "'Lo, girlie."

"You're really wasting effort," Ursula assured her. "We're so much more powerful than you are."

Fernie cried out, "Who are you?"

"Why, we're the escaped shadow criminals, of course. Us and our old friend Nebuchadnezzar back there were all busted out at the same time. We're old partners, what I suppose you would call a gang—and no mere person of flesh and blood could ever defeat one of us, let alone all four! Why don't you just give up and come with us? I promise you, life as a slave isn't nearly as bad as its reputation."

Fernie had seconds to figure out what she was going to do, if she was going to do anything at all.

She still wasn't sure what she was going to do when she skidded to a stop.

The three pursuing shadows hadn't expected that. They shot past her, though not nearly as far as Fernie would have liked. As they looped around, not in any particular hurry, Carlin remarked, "You know, I think that's the first one ever that actually did give up."

"I know," Otis said sadly. "Takes the fun out of the whole thing."

But Fernie had not given up at all. She leaped to one of the hallway's many doors, seized the big brass knocker, and rapped it hard against the wood.

The sound was slightly louder than it should have been, given how hard she knocked. It sounded a little like a sledgehammer smashing in the roof of a car. In most situations she would have said that it was altogether too loud. Today it didn't sound even remotely loud enough. Under the circumstances, she would have liked a sound like a battleship hitting the ground after being dropped from skyscraper height.

Nor did she wait to see if anybody answered her knock. Even as the shadow criminals charged her again, she raced across the hall and used the knocker on another door.

"You insufferable girl!" Ursula cried. "You really think this is going to—"

The first door Fernie had knocked on opened and the shadow of a burly man with a sloping forehead and arms like tree trunks stumbled into the hallway. "Here now! What's all the fuss?"

The shadow named Carlin stopped before him, warning him, "Don't interfere, good sir! The girl's fate is none of your concern!"

"I'm not interfering, you silly twit! I'm just answering my door!"

Ursula spread her lovely arms wide and grabbed at Fernie, who dropped to her knees, crossed the corridor in a somersault, and leaped to her feet long enough to use the knocker on yet another door.

Behind her, the second door Fernie had knocked on opened, and the shadow of a frail old woman protested, "Is this important? I'm watching my stories."

Fernie yelled, "Please! Somebody help me!"

"I really don't want to get involved," the old woman's shadow fretted.

Carlin told the burly shadow, "Just who do you think you're calling a silly twit, you twit?"

A familiar distant rumble, a lot like thunder, made the hallway shake, rattling the chandeliers and freezing both shadow criminals and shadow innocent bystanders in their tracks. It didn't freeze Fernie, who darted to yet another door and used its knocker as well, not sticking around for even a heartbeat to see who answered.

"Maaaa!" whined the kind of little boy who forever marks himself as impossibly annoying just by the way he says *Maaaa*. "There are people at the door for you!"

"What's that?" questioned the old woman. "You say you're the mailman?"

"I'm calling *you* a twit!" exploded the burly man. "You twit!"

Ursula had already found the increasingly confusing crowd of shadows more distraction than she wanted to deal with. "Get the girl! Stop her from knocking on any more doors!"

She gave the order too late, because Fernie had already knocked on another that opened to reveal the shadow of a wild-haired lady wearing a bathrobe and thick magnifying-glass eyeglasses—who didn't even seem to notice when twenty shadow cats of different sizes raced yowling into the hallway.

Otis happened to be flying past the shadow cat lady's door at that moment, just low enough to attract the natural cat instinct to leap at flying objects. A dozen of them attached themselves to his legs, belly, and face, and brought him crashing to the floor.

"'Ey! What the—?" he cried. "What a revoltin' development this is!"

Fernie zigzagged from one side of the hallway to the other, knocking twice on each door before racing to the next. The corridor grew deafening with the sounds of shadow women protesting the treatment of their cats, shadow cats yowling as Otis tried to pull them off him, shadow brats telling their unseen mothers that there seemed to be a party going on in the hallway, shadow burly men calling Carlin a twit, and Ursula screaming at everybody and everything that the little girl was getting away.

The pandemonium only grew worse as Fernie knocked on even more doors, working her way back down the corridor to the place where she'd last seen her shadow in battle with the shape-changing Nebuchadnezzar. She even added to the growing noise level herself by yelling, "Hold on, Pearlie! I'm coming back for you!"

But the single greatest noise in a space now overwhelmed with noise was that distant rumbling thunder, which she now began to realize wasn't all that distant anymore, as each fresh drumbeat rattled the chandeliers and shook flakes of plaster from the ceiling.

Far, far up ahead—farther even than the place where she could make out her own shadow, still battling Nebuchadnezzar but losing—the distant reaches of the hallway were already turning dark as a monster the size of a house charged, its massive head shattering chandelier after chandelier.

The tyrannosaur was back.

CHAPTER NINE
AN UNFRIENDLY CHAT WITH NEBUCHADNEZZAR

The pounding drumbeat Fernie heard was the sound the tyrannosaur made as it ran—and here it could run at full speed, since this corridor was so much wider and taller than the one it had smashed into rubble before.

The tyrannosaur's sudden reappearance ahead of her seemed even more unfair than anything else that had happened to Fernie tonight. It was already more than enough for her to have to deal with prison breaks, shadow criminals, shadow cat ladies, and flooded staircases, not to mention a missing father, sister, and best friend. She really didn't need a giant rampaging dinosaur on top of all that. That was just one touch too many.

With the tyrannosaur up ahead, racing toward her, Fernie wanted nothing more than to turn around and run back into the chaos she had left by knocking on so many doors; but as Fernie considered that, she took note of a sight between her and that charging beast: Nebuchadnezzar tossing her heroic shadow aside like a piece of trash to dart back inside the room where Pearlie was being held prisoner.

Fernie had no choice but to continue running toward the tyrannosaur if she hoped to reach Pearlie before Nebuchadnezzar could carry out whatever he had in mind.

There was a sudden flash of white as something just as terrible caught up with her. Ursula appeared beside her, floating in the air in no particular hurry, the white folds of her gown trailing behind her like streamers. A snarl twisted her graceful features, turning them even darker and colder as she said, "Nasty, nasty, uncooperative little girl."

Ursula's long, elegant fingernails shifted, becoming shapes like crescent moons, each of which ended in a point as razor-sharp as anything Fernie had ever seen.

Just up ahead, the now profoundly irritated tyrannosaur bellowed as it smashed another chandelier with its forehead. It spotted Fernie and darted forward, its powerful pounding feet making the floor shake with every step. *"Fernie What! I'm coming for you!"*

Everything depended on Fernie not only evading Ursula's claws but also reaching the open doorway of the room where Pearlie was being held while it was still between her and the approaching tyrannosaur.

Ursula slashed at Fernie, her claws slicing the air between them with a terrifying, audible *whoosh*.

Fernie couldn't spare the time to aim for the doorway. She could only dodge Ursula's slash and hope that her back hit the open doorway and not a wall. Her shoulder slammed into a doorjamb and she spun, sure she was dead, until she slipped through the open door and fell flat on her back.

Above her a floating Ursula, still terribly beautiful despite all her malice, hung framed in the light of the hall . . . but unfortunately *inside* the threshold, out of the charging dinosaur's way.

"Well, well, well." Ursula drifted into the dark room, her claws growing as long and terrible as curved swords. The long folds of her gown trailed into the hallway after her, as if blown by some unfelt wind. "Now that we've gotten your foolish attempt to resist out of the way, perhaps we can—"

Fernie's shadow, still intent on protecting

her, flew into the room and yanked hard on the white folds of Ursula's gown. Ursula flew backward into the hallway and into the shadow girl's embrace, when the massive foot of the tyrannosaur came down on them both.

For a moment Fernie was sure that her brave shadow had just been killed, even if that made no sense to her; Gustav had told her that shadows could not be killed, and even if that wasn't so, she couldn't see how being swept away by a bigger and more powerful shadow could kill another. But then she realized that she could hear the screams of both her shadow and Ursula receding in the distance as the tyrannosaur swept everything before it away with the force of its forward charge. The tyrannosaur didn't seem to be able to stop its charge right away— it didn't even seem to know that Fernie had evaded it by ducking into the open door. It did, however, keep yelling, "I'm coming to get you, Fernie!"

Even as its thunderous footsteps receded into the distance, the hallway echoed with the cries of the shadows trapped in its path. Fernie's shadow was among them, yelling, "Don't worry, Fernie! I'll find you again!"

But so was Ursula, snarling, "Not before I get her, you little witch!"

For a moment Fernie resented so many shadows yelling that they were either going to get her or save her, as if she wasn't a perfectly competent person all by herself and didn't have a little input of her own over whether she would be "gotten" or "saved" or not. It would have been nice just to be consulted.

But then a swarm of other terrified voices, the voices of all the other shadows milling about in the hallway, overwhelmed theirs.

"Oh, no!"

"Who let that thing loose?"

"Run away! Run awaaaay!"

"Otis! You idiot! Don't play with it!"

"Owwwww!"

"I still say you're a bunch of twits!"

"Help! Somebody—anybody! HELP!"

"Gee, this'll take forever to clean up!"

The tyrannosaur's angry bellow and the pounding sound of its footsteps trailed off into silence, as did the sound of shattering chandeliers.

This left Fernie free to deal with Nebuchadnezzar.

She rolled over onto her belly and rose up off the floor to confront him. Pearlie was no longer in the chair, but had been dragged over to the bookcase, which had now been slid open to reveal a secret passage. Only Pearlie's unmoving legs emerged from the passage to still lie inside the room. For some reason, Pearlie's legs didn't seem to cast a shadow . . . but the whereabouts of Pearlie's shadow remained a mystery.

Nebuchadnezzar, who had made himself look a little like Gustav again, floated by the opening, a vicious grin too big for a human mouth splitting his features from ear to ear.

"Poor Fernie," he sang. "You shouldn't have made it *personal*."

Fernie had to keep talking until she came up with a plan. "How did I make it personal?" she demanded. "By running? Was I *not* supposed to run?"

"Don't be a silly little brat. Everybody tries to run. My partners and I don't take that personally. It's what makes hunting humans *fun*. No, you made it personal the first time we met, when I was still locked in that terrible cell and took the shape of a helpless little girl, offering you my friendship. You made it personal for me because you said no and left me there to rot. Do you have any idea how rude that was?"

"I have an idea," Fernie said. "I also know how smart it was."

"Oh, certainly. As you so cleverly figured out back then, I had no real interest in being your friend. Had you listened to my sad story and released me from my cell, I would have disposed of you as quickly and unpleasantly as possible and then gone back to doing what got me locked up in the first place." The jagged grin grew wider. "The difference, Fernie, is that by making it *personal*, you gave me reason, other than my current employer's plans for you, to take you alive, so you can live a long and miserable life witnessing the horrible fate you've brought upon your family."

Fernie was still trying to figure out what to do. "Gee," she said with a calm she didn't feel. "Would it help if I said I was sorry?"

This surprised him. "Does that strike you as something you're likely to say?"

"Frankly, no. But you've made such a big fuss about how personal I've made this that I almost feel bad about it. How about I apologize, you give me my family back, and we forget the whole thing?"

Nebuchadnezzar looked amazed. "And you really expect that to work?"

"Nope. Not really. But it's worth a shot, I guess."

Behind him, Pearlie's legs shifted.

Was she waking up?

No.

She was being dragged.

Somebody standing behind the door had taken hold of her arms to pull her deeper into the passage . . . somebody who softly chuckled now, out of pleasure at capturing his prize.

Pearlie's legs swung up off the floor, as whoever it was got a better grip on her and picked her up, hauling her out of sight. For a moment the red balloon, which had been hidden by the door, bobbed into sight . . . but then it was yanked away, too, and both girl and balloon were gone.

It was a horrible thing for Fernie to see, but even more horrible was the awareness that Nebuchadnezzar still stood between herself and her sister, and that there was very little she could do to get past him. She formed her hands into fists. "Give her back."

"I almost wish I could," Nebuchadnezzar said mournfully. "The lot of you are really more trouble than you're worth. But I'm not the only person who takes what you've done personally. My new employer does, too. And *he* wants your entire family thrown into the Pit, not just *some* of you."

The Pit was one of the worst places in Gustav's house, a bottomless well that served as the portal to the Dark Country. People thrown in there survived the fall but were doomed to wander a place where no human being had ever been meant to live, and were as often as not taken as slaves by Lord Obsidian. Fernie and Pearlie had come close to that terrible fate once before, courtesy of one of Obsidian's nastier minions, a very bad man whom she knew only as the People Taker.

The mere thought of her family being exposed to that awful doom a second time was so heartbreaking that there were only two possible ways Fernie could have taken it: with total stunned paralysis, or with an anger deep enough to bury her fear someplace that fueled her determination to fight.

Fernie reacted the second way. She took a step toward him. "You can't have us."

"I beg to differ. We took your father first. We

have your sister now. Pretty soon we'll have you. Your mother's not all that important, as she's been away for so long that she's never committed the offenses that the rest of you have . . . but I wager that she'll come running back home from wherever she is as soon as she finds out that the rest of you have disappeared, and we'll be able to get her, too. In fact, if you're very, very lucky, Lord Obsidian will be kind and allow you all to work chained side by side—though that will not be nice for you, Fernie, as I guarantee that your parents and sister will all soon come to hate you for being the one to introduce them all to the dangers of this house."

This was just about the worst thing that anybody could have ever said to her. It stung Fernie in a way that few things could, and made her eyes burn the way eyes do when they're about to fill with tears . . . but she would not let herself cry in front of him. "My family won't hate me," she promised, the words sounding empty in her mouth. "They'll love me more, because I'm going to save them."

"Oh," Nebuchadnezzar said lazily, "I'm certain that's what you'd like to believe. In fact, it's that kind of silly thinking that will make sure you stupidly deliver yourself into our hands. So in order to make sure that happens, let's make you a solemn promise, hmm? Let's say right here and now that we *won't* throw your father and sister into the Pit until we can have all three of you in that room at the same time. My employer said there was a game he wanted to play with you there, anyway. That'll make *sure* you come to us."

That did it. The anger that had ebbed when he threatened to make sure she lost her family's love now took over again, and she charged.

Something very strange happened to him in the heartbeat it took her to cross the room. His confident, jagged smile faltered, and his eyes widened. The false Gustav Gloom face he'd been wearing seemed to melt off him all at once, replaced by the blank gray most shadows looked like when their faces could not be seen.

He shouted, "No!"

Fernie had no idea what she possibly could have done to frighten him when she had no plan more sophisticated than wading in and swinging her fists. But that moment of fear gave her strength and hope as she found herself upon him, hurling the single angriest blow of her life.

Her fist went right through his head without seeming to do anything to disturb it. The air there turned out to be far colder than the rest of the room; it was like dunking her hand in ice water, or leaving her gloves at home on a freezing day.

Even so, he seemed genuinely afraid of her. He retreated, darting through the open panel into the secret passage, and she took his flight as encouragement, prepared to chase him not only there but to the ends of the earth if that's what it took to get her father and sister back.

But then a familiar voice behind her cried, "No, Fernie! Don't! It's not you he's frightened of! It's me!"

Fernie froze in place, suddenly unsure what to do.

Nebuchadnezzar took advantage of her hesitation, not only slipping inside the passage but doing something as he went that made the bookcase slide shut and latch.

Fernie leaped on the bookshelf and pounded on it, shouting at the top of her lungs: *"Pearlie! Listen to me! Don't listen to them, and don't be afraid! I'm not going to let this happen to you! Do you hear me, Pearlie? I'm not going to let this happen to you!"*

She was still pounding the shelves, to no avail, when the owner of the familiar voice crossed the room and stood beside her, anger darkening his pale features to a shade that came very close to approaching pink.

"Neither will I," said the real Gustav Gloom.

CHAPTER TEN
GUSTAV SAYS "OW"

What happened next may have been because Fernie was so furious, she needed someplace to put her anger.

Or it could have been because she was so mixed up between real Gustavs and imposter Gustavs and emergency whistles that didn't summon any useful help and an entire band of evil shadows with names like Carlin and Ursula and Otis and Nebuchadnezzar that she had no idea what to do.

On the other hand, it might have been because she had good reason to be upset with Gustav by now and knew exactly what she was doing.

She whirled, clapped her hands onto his shoulders, and gave him a hard shove.

He didn't even try to stay upright. He just

fell on his back, landing with a loud *whump* and a gigantic cloud of billowing dust.

"Ow," he pointed out.

Fernie was mortified but didn't have the time to muster the necessary apology. "Gustav, they just took my sister—"

He held both his hands before him, palms out. "I know. I saw. But I was right to keep you from following him into that passage. It's what he wanted you to do, and it wouldn't have worked out at all well for you or your sister."

"But we can't just let them *take* her!"

"Sure we can," said Gustav, and then before she could get more upset at him than she already was, added, "in fact, that ship has sailed. We just won't let them *keep* her, or your dad, one second longer than we have to. Is it safe for me to get up now?"

She wasn't sure she could promise that, but she extended her hand.

He clasped it and allowed her to help him rise to his feet, dusting himself off as soon as he was upright. His black suit had suffered some damage since she'd seen him last: His right sleeve had been torn off at the elbow, revealing the dusty white sleeve beneath. There were other rips on his lapels, and a large one, fortunately not as noticeable as it could have been, in the seat of his pants. He'd also lost his little black shoes and his little red tie. Every part of him was covered with a layer of gray dust and glittery powdered glass.

As much as she wanted to know where he'd been and how this whole sorry situation had come to pass, she couldn't bear to stand there and watch him brushing the dust off the remains of his clothing. "Gustav," she begged. "We have to hurry—"

"It's not about hurrying," he said. "It's about *not wasting any time*. They want you so worried about Pearlie and your dad that you rush right in without giving any thought to how you're going to save them. That's a good way to make sure that they get you, too."

"But the Pit—"

"I know. I heard. I also heard Nebuchadnezzar say that his boss is not going to throw them in until he gets to play his game with all three of you. I can guarantee you that's just the kind of promise he's going to try to keep, because—as he pointed out—it's also exactly what's going to deliver you to him. That gives us time to come up with a plan." Satisfied that he had freed himself of as much of the dust as he was going to be able to, he looked at her, and with considerable difficulty, twisted his serious little lips into the closest he could come to a smile. "Trust me."

It was the last thing he ever should have said to her after the kind of night she was having. Before he knew it, he was back on the floor, once again on his back.

"Ow," he repeated, a little more insistently this time. After a moment, he complained, "You said it was safe."

"So did you!" she snapped.

It took him a second to realize what she was talking about. "Oh. My promise to your dad."

"Yes. Your promise to my dad."

"I'm sorry about that," he said humbly. "I told you, I checked out every single step of the way. I installed those safety railings and arranged other precautions wherever I could. We should have been okay."

"Why weren't we?"

He seemed hurt. "Fernie, there's a limit to how much anything, anywhere in the world, even on your side of the fence, can ever be *safe*. Your own house can be as safe as any house in any neighborhood ever, and you can promise any friend who comes over to visit that nothing's going to happen, but that doesn't mean you can guarantee that a meteor won't suddenly come plunging down from outer space and make the whole neighborhood a crater two miles deep. It doesn't mean you broke your promise. It means that you can't ever really plan for *everything*."

This somehow sounded like cheating to Fernie. "You took my family to a prison and didn't plan for a prison break?"

"Not one like this," he said.

She just stared down at him, unable to come up with a proper reply to that. "That's a pretty big mistake, Gustav."

"I can see that, and I'm so sorry that I could spend the whole night apologizing. Can I ask you something, though? I showed up in time to see that Nebuchadnezzar disguised himself as me, but I don't get why you ever believed him. You must have seen that he was only a shadow."

"He told me that he was you, *turned into* a shadow."

"Why would you even believe such a silly thing?"

She exploded. "Gustav, I don't know all the

rules of this crazy house! It *all* seems silly to me! I don't always know what makes sense here and what doesn't!"

He thought about that for a long time and finally nodded. "Okay. Are you going to push me over again? Because if you are, I'd rather not waste my time getting up."

Exasperated, she extended her hand again.

He took it, once again allowed her to pull him to his feet, and this time satisfied himself with one or two quick brushes before saying, "Come on. We need to get out of sight before Ursula and the others get back."

He led her into the hallway, which was no longer the elegant place it had been only a few minutes earlier. The walls were battered and dented, the floor covered with a layer of shattered crystal from the overhead chandeliers. Burning candles had fallen and started small flickering fires. Everywhere Fernie looked, shadows flattened by the tyrannosaur's charge resentfully peeled themselves off the floor while complaining about how long it was going to take them to clear away all the rubble. It generally looked like somebody had gone on a joy ride with a bulldozer, and then carefully backed up to make sure he succeeded in crushing anything that had somehow remained intact.

Fernie also realized that her own shadow was missing. "Gustav, is my shadow dead?"

"Why would she be dead?"

"She was with Ursula when the tyrannosaur ran by."

"Shadows can't be hurt that way. She probably got swept away with the rest of them. Don't worry. Sooner or later she'll find her way back to you. With any luck, sooner. We could use her help."

Fernie was reassured. "Good." But that, of course, only answered some of her questions, because she now saw that Gustav was missing his shadow, too. "Where's yours?"

"On an errand," Gustav said.

She hardly knew which one of her million and one questions to ask next. "What happened after you and my dad went into the Hall of Shadow Criminals?"

He picked his way through the rubble, his stocking feet moving across the field of broken glass without ever being cut by it. "We were okay for a little while. Your dad wasn't happy walking on those pathways with all the big empty spaces between them, but he did admit that the safety railings Hives installed made the walk perfectly safe as far as he could see. Just before the trouble started, he agreed to come back for you two so I could take you to speak to Hieronymus Spector."

He opened his mouth and then closed it, as if unsure whether he should say the next part.

"What?"

"We talked a little bit on the way back. Your dad told me that he was sorry about the family having to move away. He also said that he wished he could take me with you, and that if he ever had a chance, he would be proud to make me a permanent part of your family. It wasn't the first time he's said something like that, but . . ." He bit his lip, as if considering three or four different places the sentence could go from there. "Anyway. We were almost back to the door when the emergency sirens started. I don't know if you could hear them outside where you were, but inside the prison they were as loud as anything I've ever heard; there's never been an escape from the Hall of Shadow Criminals for as long as I've been alive, so it's the first time I've heard them. I had no idea what to do.

"Then shadows started coming up through

the empty spaces between the paths . . . ummm, here. This is as good a shortcut as any."

The door looked like every other door in sight, except that it was a shade of yellow and bore a disgusting green stain on it. He opened it now, ushered her in, and led her through a dim room filled with chairs: easy chairs, high chairs, dentist's chairs, airplane seats, recliners, hundreds of them, all of them lopsided and melted, as if they'd been made of wax and then exposed to extreme heat.

He said, "This, by the way, is the Hall of—"

"I don't need to know, Gustav. Just finish the story you already started."

"Okay," he said, not at all upset that he had to skip the explanation for all the chairs. "So I told you once before that the empty spaces between the walkways in the Hall of Shadow Criminals drop all the way down to the Dark Country. I also told you that they hang over a very bad part of the Dark Country where even shadows don't live. It's a long distance from anyplace useful, which is probably why nobody ever considered Lord Obsidian mounting an attack from that direction.

"But that's what happened. There were

hundreds of them, all so dark I couldn't tell whether they were the shadows of men or women, coming up out of the emptiness and climbing up onto the walkways between us and the exit.

"Your dad, who doesn't understand the way things work in this house any more than you do, asked me, 'Is this normal?' I had to tell him it wasn't, even as the invaders started crying out, 'Free the prisoners! Free the prisoners! Free the prisoners for Lord Obsidian!'

"I was afraid at first that they wanted to free *all* the prisoners, because that would have meant freeing Hieronymus Spector and a couple of others almost as bad as him who would have proceeded straight to the world outside the fence and caused suffering greater than you can possibly imagine, but no; while Lord Obsidian might want to free those shadows someday, they don't seem to have been on the list of prisoners he wanted freed today. Today he only wanted to free the ones you've met."

Fernie broke in. "Nebuchadnezzar, Carlin, Ursula, and Otis."

Gustav nodded. "Yes. The Four Terrors."

The two friends had reached the back wall of the room with all the chairs. Gustav opened the door there, revealing a narrow, unfinished hallway Fernie recognized as part of the network of servant passages that ran behind all the house's main rooms.

Gustav led her through the dim space, his features visible only when he passed through one of the shafts of light shining down through the cracks in the upper floors.

He went on: "The Four Terrors are infamous, Fernie. My shadow mother used to tell me scary stories about them when I was small. Even Great-Aunt Mellifluous warned me against them. She used to tell me that it was shadows like the Four Terrors, and the evil they do, that make the world of light spend so much energy confusing dark things for evil things, as if one always means the same thing as the other. It doesn't, you know. It never has. Some of the most wonderful things you can think of happen in dark places, and some of the worst evils committed in your own world are committed in daylight, under a bright sun, in places where everybody can see them happening.

"I don't know where the Four Terrors came from, or what happened to make them so evil, but a long time ago, they roamed the world of people, causing misery and ruining lives just for the sheer fun of it. The one I found you talking to, Nebuchadnezzar, was their leader. He could change his shape, and he amused himself by appearing before human beings, turning them against their friends and loved ones, or causing wars where brother fought against brother. He's most famous, I think, for appearing before a young Danish prince and talking the poor gullible kid into believing that his uncle had killed his father. That caused a mess you wouldn't believe. Don't get me started on that story, or I'll be talking all day.

"Anyway, Carlin and Ursula were his lieutenants; they were in charge of charming people, getting them to do whatever terrible things Nebuchadnezzar wanted them to do. Entire pointless wars started because of them, Fernie. You can track a lot of the evil things people have done to one another to their influence.

"As for Otis, he wasn't very smart, but he knew a hundred ways a shadow could hurt a person, and about fifty ways that a shadow could kill one. You hear stories about boogeymen sometimes. They're not all about Otis, of course. But he contributed to more than his share of them.

He . . ." Gustav was silent for several seconds. "It's terrible, Fernie. It's more terrible than you should ever have to hear. It's more terrible even than I want to say. Will you be able to accept that much if I also tell you that we'll do whatever we can to save your family?"

Her heart felt cramped. "You can skip the horror stories about all the terrible things the Four Terrors have done. I know they're bad. I could hardly miss that part. Just tell me what happened to my father."

Gustav slumped a little, as if suddenly feeling a terrible weight that he'd managed to forget for a little while, but now he spoke faster, racing through the words even as he moved faster to race through the passage. "All right. Lord Obsidian's shadow army was all around us, blocking our way back to you and flying in waves to the cells holding the Four Terrors. Those cells, like the others, they were made of light so pure that it's impossible for even the most powerful shadow criminal locked inside one to get out, or for even the most powerful friend of a shadow criminal to get in. Any shadows who try to pass through those cell walls, either in or out, sizzle away to nothingness.

"It's a terrible thing to see, Fernie, and an even more terrible thing to hear. No single shadow could survive it.

"But Obsidian had hundreds of shadows to spend, and they were all willing to sacrifice themselves in order to free the Terrors. They didn't just fly to the four cages. They *swarmed* over those four cages like ants, evaporating by the dozen only to be replaced by more just as willing to give their lives for what their master wanted." He shook his head. "Fernie, it took less time to happen than it does to say. The light of those four cages started to dim. I realized that all the light was being used up, and told your dad, 'We're in big trouble. We have to get out of here now.'

"He said, 'How?' Which was a good question, because there were more reinforcements coming up through the darkness with every second. Already, the path between us and the main entrance was filled with them. They didn't seem to be at all interested in us yet, but I wasn't willing to take your dad through all of that, not when it looked like the Four Terrors were going to be free at any minute.

"So I said, 'Fernie and I found another way

out the last time we visited. We have to go out that way and make our way back to the girls as fast as we can.'

"He didn't want to go. He said, 'But what are they going to do if we're not back in time?'

"There was no time to argue with him, because that's when Nebuchadnezzar got out. I heard him yelling above all the war cries of Obsidian's army, 'Those humans over there! Don't let them get away!'

"Some of them did come after us, Fernie, but only a few of them, at the start; I think what saved us from being buried by the lot of them is that they were still obeying Obsidian's orders to free the Four Terrors and didn't see why they should start listening to orders from anybody else before they were done. But if we were going to run away at all, we had to run away that moment. So I tugged your dad's wrist and told him that if he ever wanted to see you or Pearlie again, he had to follow me. It took him a second to obey, but even he could see that there was no choice, and ran after me.

"Behind us we heard Carlin shout that he was free, and then we heard the same from Otis, and finally from Ursula. We put as much distance between us and them as we could, but the walkways in the Hall form a labyrinth, as you know, and that meant we sometimes had to double back and run *toward them* instead of away.

"If your dad's concerns hadn't made me install all those safety railings, we could have jumped the gaps. But the safety railings kept us from doing that. It did help a lot that there were, by now, only a few of Obsidian's soldiers left—he'd known exactly how many he had to use up—but that still left us with the Four Terrors to deal with. They were catching up with us faster than I could ever believe, and your dad wasn't having a good time with all that running.

"I guess I never realized before now, never having known my dad, that dads can run out of breath before kids do, and might have to start slowing down even while there are still monsters chasing them. Ursula was right behind him, reaching for him with her sharpened claws, when he barely managed to get out the words, 'Gustav! Don't worry about me! Get Fernie and Pearlie out of the house!'

"I didn't want to leave him behind, Fernie. I really didn't. He's not my dad, but he's *a* dad, and since meeting him, I've hoped that he's the kind of man my dad turns out to be. But even as I turned around, I saw Otis take him by the arms and Carlin take him by the legs, while Ursula knelt on his shoulders, weighing him down. It didn't stop your dad, who was so determined to keep running that he managed to keep it up for a little while, even with the three of them hanging onto him and trying to bring him down.

"I was in trouble, too. Some of Lord Obsidian's remaining soldiers had caught up to me. There were at least a dozen of them, all at once. They got my tie and my shoes, and were still struggling with me as your dad fell down; I must have looked pretty beaten myself, because the Terrors just let the others continue to tear at me as Nebuchadnezzar, who had made himself look like the shadow of a little girl, arrived.

"Unfortunately, he had heard your dad mention your name, and it meant something to him. He cried, 'Fernie? Really? This worthless old man is Fernie's father? The Fernie I know? The Fernie I've been asked to get? And she's in the house now? How convenient is that?'

"Ursula said, 'This is going to be easy!'

"Nebuchadnezzar transformed in midair,

turning himself into a version of me. 'You take care of the man and the halfsie boy. I'll go find the stupid girls.'

"Carlin said, 'Are you going to need any help dealing with them?'"

Gustav hesitated, looking like he would have preferred eating tacks to saying the next part. "I'm sorry, Fernie. This next part is not my opinion. It's his.

"Nebuchadnezzar laughed. 'The little one's clever enough, in her animal manner—I learned that the hard way, to my sorrow—but she's not one tenth as smart as she thinks she is. She's as stupid as any other naive little girl. She was never going to amount to anything in her life, anyway. And I'm sure her sister's not any better. Don't worry, I've heard enough about this halfsie freak over the years to keep them fooled until I've brought them both to ruin. Just catch up with me as soon as you have the other two stored away. We have a schedule to keep.'

"That's when your dad yelled at them. He was out of breath, Fernie, but he managed to say it all. 'My daughters are smarter than all of you put together, you monsters! And what smarts they don't have, this boy has! I promise you, messing around with them is the worst mistake you've ever made! We'll all be sleeping in our own beds tonight!' They went to shut him up, but then he looked me in the eyes and shouted, 'Gustav! Go!' So I threw off the shadows wrestling with me . . . and left him behind."

Gustav stopped in midstep to cover his face with his hands. Fernie almost ran into his back. She could barely see, because it was dark and her tears made everything a blur, but she hadn't expected Gustav to be affected the same way. She knew enough about him to recognize some of what she saw as shame, and found that she didn't want to hear any more of his story. "But he was alive when you saw him last, right?"

"He was alive," Gustav echoed.

"And they hadn't taken him down to the Dark Country yet."

"No," Gustav said, shaking. "They hadn't."

"So that's something."

"Yes," Gustav said. "It's something."

But from the way the courage seemed to have gone out of him all at once, he still wasn't done.

Fernie found herself afraid that he'd held back the worst part, something so terrible that it would make all the horrors they'd experienced so far seem small. Maybe they'd hurt her father in some way. She couldn't bear to know, but she couldn't bear not knowing, either. She couldn't keep the quaver out of her voice. "Gustav? What is it?"

When he turned to look at her, she saw that while no tears had escaped his eyes, there was still a flood of them, refusing to well over and stream down his cheeks.

He pointed at her face. "Fernie, I live in a shadow house, where miracles happen in every room, every day. Despite all the crazy things I've had to live with, all the impossibilities I've had to get used to, I've never, ever heard or seen anything as wonderful as that thing he said to them. Don't you ever dare think, even for a moment, that your father doesn't believe in you. He believes in you more than I've ever been lucky enough to have anybody believe in me."

Understanding his problem now, she took his wrist and moved the pointing finger away from her face. Then she said, "You know, Gustav, I really don't think you've been paying enough attention to anything my family's been telling you."

He blinked. It was the kind of blink that makes eyes that have been trying not to overflow with tears release great soggy floods. Maybe if the predicament the two friends were in had not been quite this serious, his eyes would have done just that. But it *was* this serious, and there was nothing tears could do to help. So he blinked, and when he was done blinking, the tears were gone, replaced with the calm determination Fernie had long since grown used to seeing from Gustav Gloom.

He squared his shoulders. "All right, then. Let's go get your family."

CHAPTER ELEVEN
THE SHADOW WHO RUINED MOVIE NIGHT

About ten minutes later, the two friends emerged from the servant passages into a vast and elegant gallery with walls of carved dark wood, ornate oriental carpets so beautiful that they dazzled despite the usual ankle-deep layer of gray mist obscuring them, tempting easy chairs arranged in circles around coffee tables, and what looked like hundreds of paintings, ranging in size from some smaller than Fernie's thumb to others large enough to decorate the sides of barns.

It wasn't the first art gallery Fernie had found in Gustav's home, but the last one had been all portraits, and this one presented a variety of images, from bloody battlefields to grinning elderly ladies.

There was also a painting of a horrid old skeletal castle of black stone, rising from a black swamp to stand tall and foreboding against a starless black sky. There was even black lightning, crashing against the black night. All around the castle, dark inhuman armies, numbering thousands, stood in formation, knee-deep in the muck, some not wearing shoes or not much caring that any shoes they wore would be peeled off by the mud the second they tried to take a step.

With all the black set against other shades of black in a place composed of so many shades of darkness, there seemed no possible way that anything in the picture should have been visible at all—but it was somehow all perfectly clear, a place that had never known light but which was too stubborn to let its ebony majesty go unseen.

There were some human beings in sight: men, women, and children, all skinny, all dressed in rags, all identifiable at first glance as slaves. They had the miserable look of people who have been frightened for so long that they no longer know how to be anything else. Some of them were being dragged along the ground like shadows, by shadows who walked upright like men.

Gustav saw Fernie stop to stare at the terrible image, and put a hand on her shoulder. "That's Lord Obsidian's palace."

Fernie shivered. "That's what it looks like in the Dark Country?"

"Yes," Gustav said. "But that's not a painting of the Dark Country. This is the Gallery of Possible Futures, where all the paintings are images of things that might someday come to be. That's one possible future for your world, if Lord Obsidian ever gets his way. It's not a palace that stands now. It's a palace he wants to build."

Fernie could hardly bear the thought. "But why would he want it, Gustav? He used to be a person, back when he was called Howard Philip October. What could possibly go wrong with somebody, even an evil somebody, that would cause him to want to make the world look like *that*?"

Gustav shrugged. "Maybe his mom and dad didn't hug him enough. Maybe he didn't get what he wanted for his birthday one year. Maybe he never learned how to keep his clothes from clashing and wanted to simplify things by getting rid of every color except black. And maybe he's just a big evil bully who wants to wipe out all happiness, everywhere, because it strikes him as a fun thing to do."

"What do you think?"

"I don't think it matters much. It only matters that he's a real stinker."

They moved on, past more paintings of things that might come to be: bright shiny futures with jet packs and rocket cars and starships zipping around from one solar system to another, strange futures where dolphins walked around on two legs while leading obedient human beings on leashes, immediately upsetting futures with the Gloom house engulfed in flames, and futures easily as disastrous as the one where Lord Obsidian had conquered all, except with catastrophes of different kinds, like wars and falling asteroids.

Fernie decided that she didn't like this room very much. "Are there any paintings where you and I rescue my father and sister, and we all live happily ever after?"

"I'm sure there are," Gustav said. "This room is like every other gallery in the house; there's more to see than you could possibly get to in a lifetime, and you can always find what you're looking for if you look hard enough. But why would you even want to spend time looking for such a thing now?"

"I don't know. Maybe because it would make me feel better."

"I'm sure it would. It would make me feel better, too. But it wouldn't mean that what you see is going to come true." He thought a minute. "It's like . . . well, you can't see it as one of those fairy tales they tell kids, where the princess finds a prophecy telling her how everything's going to work out for the best . . . or the worst. There are no prophecies in real life. There's just stuff that might happen, and might not."

"Then let's try to make sure that the painting with Lord Obsidian's palace doesn't happen."

"I'm working on it," he said.

"What about saving my family?"

"I'm working on that, too," he said, and suddenly raised his voice: "Hello, Cousin Cyrus."

The shadow that rose from the ankle-deep layer belonged to a frail elderly man, who even made of flesh would have looked like he could have been bowled over by a light breeze. His bushy white eyebrows were so thick that it was impossible to make out any eyes behind them, while his dangling nose and protruding chin came very close to touching. He wore what on a human being would have been a dirty white undershirt and boxer shorts with hearts on them, and seemed genuinely put out to have his rest disturbed by the halfsie boy and outsider girl. "Durn it," he said with deep irritation. "I was hoping you wouldn't see me under the mist."

"I didn't," said Gustav. "But you always sleep in this particular spot."

"It's quiet. Nobody bothers me. I don't like to be bothered. You're the only one who comes around, asking for favors all the time."

"I've never asked you for a favor," Gustav told him. "I've only collected debts."

Cousin Cyrus harrumphed. "Any debt I owed you for the few inconsequential services you might have done for me over the years, I paid back long ago."

To Fernie's astonishment, Gustav reached into the chest pocket of his now-tattered suit and pulled out a small, worn spiral notepad, flipping past several pages to one covered with dense, spidery handwriting.

"According to the accounts," Gustav said, "you've paid me back for helping you chase away the Story Thieves, for rescuing your spirit from the Soul Bunny, and for tracking down your tiny little heart and stealing it back from the display case in Commodore Phantagore's Museum of Inexplicable Antiquities."

"That's all I owed you," Cousin Cyrus said.

Gustav was not deterred. "You didn't pay me back for that one family movie night when I was six, when you were sitting behind me and wouldn't stop playing the bagpipes during *The Princess Bride Returns*, no matter how many times my shadow mother and Great-Aunt Mellifluous begged you to stop."

"That's not a debt," Cousin Cyrus protested. "I didn't like you then any more than I like you now. I was *trying* to ruin the movie for you."

"Did you or did you not say these exact words to me after my shadow mother spent half an hour yelling at you for being so obnoxious: 'All right, all right already! Sorry, kid, I owe you one'?"

The elderly shadow opened his mouth, then closed it, then opened it, then closed it again. He suddenly looked very chagrined and very trapped. "Only a halfsie brat would remember that after so many years."

"Only a halfsie brat in desperate need of assistance would have to," said Gustav.

Still, Cousin Cyrus resisted: "Why don't you

just go to Mellifluous? That silly old woman actually *likes* you."

"She went to the Dark Country yesterday morning, on a secret mission involving the war against Lord Obsidian."

Those words surprised Fernie more than anything that had been said during the whole strange conversation. Fernie had met Great-Aunt Mellifluous a number of times and liked her quite a bit, but had never imagined her to be the kind of person who went on secret missions. She had always struck Fernie as more like the kind of person who served tea to other old ladies, talked to them about orchids, and expressed any level of surprise with the words *Oh, my*.

Amazed at this latest news about her, Fernie said, "Oh, my."

Cousin Cyrus glanced at her for the first time, looked annoyed, and then turned back to Gustav again, as if she didn't exist. "So? What does that have to do with me?"

"What it has to do with you," Gustav said, "is that the Pit to the Dark Country is probably being guarded right now by the Four Terrors or their allies. Any other shadow I sent through the portal to take a message to Great-Aunt Mellifluous would probably be stopped or taken prisoner."

"And I won't?"

"I don't see why they'd bother. You're famous for not caring about anything or anybody. Everybody knows that the person whose shape you wear was a nasty old man the world forgot about as soon as it had a chance, that you're just like him, and that you want nothing to do with either people *or* shadows. They even know that you want nothing to do with me. There's no reason they wouldn't let you through. They'd never imagine you lifting a finger to help anybody. But you still do owe me one, Cyrus, and you know what it means, in this house, to ignore a legitimate debt. So you will do this for me. You will go down to the Dark Country, you will find Great-Aunt Mellifluous at the headquarters of the Resistance Army, and you will give her my message."

A dark anger flared behind those overhanging eyebrows. It was such a cold, helpless anger that Fernie immediately gave up on all possibility of this shadow being just a crotchety old man of the sort who played at being grumpy but had enough goodness in him to do the right thing if ever given a chance. He was an enemy.

"What's your message?"

"You will tell Great-Aunt Mellifluous that Mr. What and his daughter Pearlie are in trouble. You will tell her that the Four Terrors intend to throw the two of them, and Fernie if they get her, and also probably me, into the Pit. You will tell her that we're doing everything we can to rescue them from this end, but that if we fail, she will only have a limited amount of time to act before they fall into the hands of Lord Obsidian. And finally, you will tell her that I won't be here when she gets back, because I'm going down to the Dark Country myself to rescue my father. Do you have all that?"

Cousin Cyrus's snarl grew wider, developing fangs. "I have it. But after this . . . we're done."

Gustav nodded. "Fine."

Cousin Cyrus roared his displeasure and flitted away, like a scrap of paper caught in a high wind. He flattened when he reached the set of double doors at the far end of the gallery, to fit through the slight seam between them, and was gone.

Gustav watched him go and visibly relaxed,

revealing only in that moment the tension that had tightened his posture for several long minutes now.

Fernie said, "That's your plan?"

"It's a backup plan," Gustav said. "In case we get killed. I'm not saying it'll be much consolation to us."

Fernie chewed on that. "No."

"Maybe we can come up with something better."

They walked on, passing a painting of two people: a tall, handsome man she thought she recognized as Gustav's father, Hans, and a beautiful redheaded woman she would have assumed to be Gustav's mother had she not once seen a picture of Penny Gloom and known her to be beautiful in a completely different way. This painting depicted Hans and the strange, unknown woman in mountain-climbing gear atop a pillar of rock with a vast brown desert far below. It looked like a terrible drop if either one of them slipped. Fernie's father would have recommended the introduction of safety railings.

But she couldn't stop thinking about Cousin Cyrus. "You know, Gustav, my own cousins are much nicer."

"I'm sure they are. But your family's all *people*. Mine aren't. It's like I've told you: Most of them think I don't belong and wouldn't lift a finger to help me. Some even hate me, and would have killed me a long time ago if I hadn't been protected by others like my shadow mother or Great-Aunt Mellifluous. I'm not saying we're in this alone; we're not. But we have to make do with the advantages we have, and," he said, pointing at the set of double doors up ahead, "we have to do that before we open those doors."

"Why? Why those doors?"

"Because they open up on a balcony overlooking the grand parlor. We're going to have to cross it in order to get to where your father and sister are being taken, and that means I can think of no *better* place for the Four Terrors to be lying in wait for us than on the other side."

"Oh," said Fernie.

Gustav said nothing as the pair of them walked toward the double doors.

Fernie had the feeling that things were going to get very bad for them very quickly as soon as those doors were opened.

Gustav moved to a cord hanging by the side of the doors, and gave it a quick yank.

Fernie felt a distant, deep vibration, like the loudest moment in the sound track of the next theater over.

Almost immediately, the hairline crack between the floor and the bottom of the door grew dark and filled with a line of utter blackness . . . blackness that flowed into the room, rose, and filled out until it became the looming figure of a familiar, scowling, spotty butler.

Hives sniffed. "I *do* hope this is worth my valuable time."

CHAPTER TWELVE
GUSTAV GOES SURFING

Twenty minutes later, Gustav Gloom left the Gallery of Possible Futures and stepped out upon the balcony alone.

His sad eyes surveyed the battleground before him with the critical view of a boy who had often needed to search the rooms of his house for the best places to evade monsters.

He was two balconies above a grand parlor teeming with activity. Down below, hundreds of shadows wandered to and fro, chattering in languages that ranged from some known to Man to others that could be formed by no human tongue. Some danced; others drifted aimlessly as if they'd traveled a long distance to get to this place and then forgotten why they'd come; a few fought duels over casual insults, their shadowy swords clanging and giving off little black sparks as the duelists shouted things like "Have at thee, sirrah!" There were also shadow paperboys hawking the latest extras about the terrible prison break at the Hall of Shadow Criminals; the headline of one within Gustav's sight read FOUR FLEE; FEAR FOLLOWS.

Some, a very few, of the house's many residents took note of Gustav as he approached the railing. They said things like "Oh, look, it's the boy." Or "I wonder what he's going to break today." Or "Just look at what he's done to that suit." Or, most unnervingly, "I wonder if he knows who's looking for him."

Gustav spent a few seconds standing at the railing and looking at the parlor's splendid collection of staircases: the short circular ones that connected some floors to the next, the sweeping ones that stretched from the ground floor to balconies ten or twenty levels higher up, the rickety ones that dangled over the parlor floor at bizarre angles, clearly treacherous because they were missing more steps than not.

On each of those levels, he knew, there were hundreds of doors, thousands of possible destinations, maybe an infinite number of places to get lost and never be seen again.

It was wonderful. It was terrible. It was home.

He spotted Ursula's familiar figure, wandering around on the floor far below; she clearly wasn't mingling, like so many of the others, but hunting, her long gray-white hair and long white gown streaming out behind her as if driven by a powerful wind that affected no other shadow in sight. She passed within sight of some of the shadows reading newspapers about her escape, but none among them seemed to notice or care, either because most shadows didn't pay much attention to current events or because they preferred to mind their own business.

He didn't see Carlin or Otis anywhere, and knew it was likely a waste of time to look for Nebuchadnezzar, who could be wearing any shape. But it was enough to have seen one of them.

So he leaned over the balcony and shouted down at her. *"Hey, you!"*

Ten thousand sets of eyes, Ursula's among them, peered up at him. Most looked away at once, muttering things like "Oh, it's just the boy." But Ursula's lips curled into a smile. It was the kind of expression that on someone else's face might have been charming, but on hers seemed to lower the temperature in the house by twenty degrees.

"Oh!" she cried. "You're giving up! How wonderfully *considerate* of you!"

Gustav gripped the railing. "I have a message for you, Ursula. For all of you."

"How sweet! Don't keep it to yourself, dear."

"You still have time to give my friends back, unharmed. After that, you can leave this house, go somewhere that doesn't have any people, and never hurt anybody again."

Her amused titter was like the chiming of little bells. "And if we don't?"

"Then," Gustav said, "in five minutes we'll all see how loudly you can scream."

Her eyes widened a little at that, but then the ridiculousness of that promise sank in, and she started to laugh . . . first with more gentle tittering, then with incredulous giggling, and finally with cruel belly laughs. Her hilarity quickly spread to many of the shadows around her. Some of them hadn't been paying attention to the conversation but just wanted to join in on the fun; others thought Gustav was every bit as silly as she did and wanted to join her in making sport of him; and a very small few, either smarter or more experienced than the others, laughed at her for not taking the little boy's dire promise with the seriousness it deserved.

She might not have laughed so long and so hard if she'd noticed just how many of the drifting shadows didn't laugh at all, but instead retreated into the many side passages rather than stay in the parlor during whatever was going to happen.

Spotting Carlin and Otis was a little like spotting a friend in the seats opposite yours at a crowded football stadium; harder, in fact, since human friends dress in different colors and have differently colored hair and do not blur together in a gray fog the way shadows do when they're all crowded together in one place. But Gustav had been raised in this house and had better eyes for spotting individual shadows than most would have ever imagined.

He'd spotted Carlin and Otis taking advantage of his exchange with Ursula to glide up a pair of stairways at opposite ends of the parlor. Even as he watched, they both reached the top of their respective staircases and turned onto the balcony, flying toward him at waist height. Carlin approached from the left, Otis from the right, both distant shapes at the ends of long, straight walkways but both moving fast enough to be on him in seconds.

Ursula started rising, her gown somehow hanging far lower than a gown should have hung on a woman her height, if she ever planned to walk around without tripping on it. Her gray-white hair flowed behind her like a banner. She, too, would be upon Gustav in heartbeats.

Gustav didn't wait. He hopped up on the railing and jumped straight up, farther than any non-halfsie boy could have jumped, grabbing the lip of the balcony above his and pulling himself up onto the next floor.

Ursula thought this hilarious. "Oh, dear! Oh, my! You think you can get away from us that way?"

"Wasn't my whole plan," said Gustav.

He climbed past ten more balconies, rising more quickly than many birds can fly. Below, Carlin and Otis had taken to flight themselves and now rose by Ursula's sides, each just a little below her.

Ursula seemed to be having the time of her life. "You're so generous with choices, dear, that we should offer you one. If you don't want us to get you, you could always just let go and fall! I promise, we won't try to catch you. It'll be worth it for us just to see you hit the ground."

"That's generous of you, too," said Gustav. "You have three minutes now."

Rather than continue to climb up, he jumped down and to the side and grabbed the railing one floor below, just long enough to alter his course and launch himself into the open space over the parlor.

Ursula had been right; a fall from this height could kill him.

But he had no intention of hitting the floor.

Instead, he landed, standing, on the polished wooden banister of one of the many staircases that crossed the atrium, and immediately started sliding straight downward, his arms extended for balance.

"That's impossible!" Carlin cried, somewhere behind him. "A boy can't do that!"

"This boy's done it plenty of times," said Gustav Gloom, adding, "it's great fun."

The staircases over the grand parlor had been Gustav's favorite jungle gym for as long as he'd lived. This trick of surfing the railings was one of his favorites. Of course, had he not already lost his shoes, he would have had to take them off. Balancing on a polished wooden railing over a fifteen-story fall is, after all, the kind of thing that really does require socks.

The lower balcony ahead of him loomed and seemed safely free of enemies—until Carlin and Otis popped up at the base of the stairs, waiting for him.

Carlin showed pointed teeth. "We have you now!"

"I don't think so," said Gustav, jumping off the side.

He landed on the railing of *another* set of stairs and began a long, swift slide in the opposite direction.

Ursula swept past him, her lunge missing him by so little that he felt the silky touch of her gown as it brushed the top of his head. The voice that had recently seemed so musical now sounded more like the ear-piercing shriek of a harpy. "You idiots! He's making a fool of you!"

"I'm not *making* anything," Gustav said as he slid toward his next destination. "I'm just bringing out what's already there. And by the way, you have two minutes now."

She howled as she and her two companions

flew down the staircase after him. Otis, first to almost catch up with him, spread his meaty arms wide and grabbed. But Gustav, acting as if he had eyes on the back of his head, leaped from that railing to the one on the other side of the stairs, and from there into open space again, landing on another nearby staircase and racing up its steps two or three at a time.

Gustav's uphill run was normally not all that much slower than his falling. He'd been raised by shadows and had won any number of games of tag with them. But his one disadvantage in such games was that he was a boy and not a shadow, and therefore capable of getting tired; he would not be able to keep this up for much longer. But he didn't *have* to keep this up for much longer.

And he was going to be given the few precious seconds he needed by the very shadows chasing him.

So he slowed to a stop and allowed himself to gasp for breath as Ursula came in for a landing five steps above him, and Carlin and Otis did the same five steps below him.

Ursula's beautiful features had seemed to melt. They hadn't been false, but they had been thin, the same way that the surface beauty of some other quite terrible people was thin; a few short minutes of frustration and rage had made her eyes widen, her lips distort into a grimace, and her jaw set like stone. Her charming face now became a hideous glare that reflected how truly awful she really was.

Even her long silky gown, as much an element of her apparent beauty as her facial features had been, had changed. The fabric now looked grayer, coarser, and filthier. There were holes in it. The edges had gone black, as if the material had been plucked from some fire where it had been set to burn because it was not anything any decent person should have ever wanted to wear.

"What was the point of all that?" she demanded. "All you managed to do was waste our time and put us to a whole lot of trouble."

Gustav held up an index finger, letting them know that he had more to say as soon as he caught his breath. He inhaled, exhaled, inhaled again, got the air he needed, and said, "But the point of it was keeping you occupied while my terrible butler, Hives, got Fernie across the grand parlor safely. And everything I told you before is still true. You still have a chance to run away and find some place far from this house where you'll never have to pay for your crimes. It's your decision."

Ursula glared at Gustav with the pure fury of a hateful creature who would have been just as happy to kill him as look at him. "I don't like threats, you despicable . . . little . . . *boy*. Otis? We don't need to keep this one. Throw him over the side."

As the hulking figure of Otis drew close behind him, Gustav shrugged. "Time's up."

High above them, something exploded.

CHAPTER THIRTEEN
THE MOST INAPPROPRIATE NICKNAME *EVER*

A staircase twenty stories above their heads chose that moment to break in half.

This was a shame, really, because it was one of the more ornate and beautiful in the mansion's considerably varied collection: a sweeping masterwork of marble stairs and beautifully sculpted wrought-iron railings, which extended from one balcony that was not fancy enough to deserve it to another that didn't even come close to being worth the journey.

The only flaw in its construction was that it was not strong enough to bear the weight of a tyrannosaur who had just leaped to one of those landings from twenty stories even higher up.

The result was a little bit like throwing a bus off the top of a tall building onto a stacked pile of clean dishes.

Not only did the marble steps shatter, not

only did the ironwork twist and snap and tumble, but the entire staircase ripped away from its two endpoints and tumbled in pieces toward the parlor floor.

On its way down, it also snapped a rickety rope bridge, which didn't slow it down at all, shattered a set of stone stairs that didn't do much better, and demolished a number of other structures, ranging from one beautiful set of mahogany stairs to one rather flimsy one made of tissue paper that was itself already covered with holes from the handful of foolish explorers who had tried to use it in the past.

Each staircase collapsed under the weight of wreckage from above, a hammering drumbeat that somehow didn't drown out the one sound louder than all the destruction: the delighted, high-pitched *"Wheeeeeeee!"* of the tyrannosaur.

Ursula craned her neck back and saw the oncoming wave of wreckage. "You intolerable little urchin! What have you *done*?"

Gustav said, "You're not the only one with powerful friends."

Otis, who had been as paralyzed by the sight of the wreckage tumbling toward them as Ursula was, made a weak grab for him . . . but Gustav had already ducked between his legs, hopped back onto the banister, and begun a swift downward slide to safety.

The hovering Carlin whirled in place as Gustav slid past him, ready to resume the chase. But then one of the first major falling objects, a stone planter from the landing of the staircase the tyrannosaur had smashed first, slammed into the path, punching a neat hole in the steps immediately before him. Carlin drew back in terror, instinctively looked up to see what might be coming next, and found his gaze drawn by the most prominent feature of the debris tumbling toward him: the gaping, fanged mouth filling his personal sky.

He managed a terrified "No!"

With a mighty gulp, the tyrannosaur snatched Carlin out of the air and swallowed him whole just before impacting the stairway headfirst. The entire structure shuddered and tore free of the balcony at its lower end, dropping ten feet on that side but somehow remaining attached to the balcony at its highest point. Gustav reached the end of his slide and leaped off, hitting the next balcony down with a somersault that ended with him back on his feet and running.

Up above, Otis was in trouble. He might have been okay if he'd been hovering like Ursula. As it happened, he'd been standing on the stairs, his full weight—or whatever shadows use for weight—on his own two feet. As the stairway dipped, he tumbled, rolling down the stairs with a cry indignant enough to inform all the shadows and human beings in earshot that he considered this moment a tremendous blow to his dignity.

The tyrannosaur, who had grabbed hold of the damaged structure with his powerful jaws, had pulled himself back up onto the steps, and now lowered his massive head to catch Otis out of the air. Otis sailed right down the creature's throat without a moment of assistance from the teeth or tongue.

The tyrannosaur stood up, shaking himself thoroughly to free his scales from some of the dust and debris. A particularly large chunk of masonry bounced off the top of his head, almost knocking him down, but he recovered, his eyes narrowing as he observed the floating figure of a beautiful woman in a gray and burned gown.

Ursula turned to flee.

A steel beam punched through the steps behind her as easily as a pencil poking through paper, and it snagged one of her gown's longer strips of silk, yanking her back in midstep.

Far below, the leading edge of the debris began to hit the grand parlor floor. The air filled with the din of a thousand screaming shadows, running for cover in every direction as hundreds of tons of wreckage slammed into the floor all around them.

Wherever the screams could be understood as words, it was clear that most of the shadows down below weren't terrified as much as loudly annoyed. The main sentiment fell in line with the exclamation of one fat shadow wearing a tuxedo, top hat, and pair of monocles (one for each eye, a pretty clear demonstration that he'd missed the whole point of monocles): "Oh, great! The boy's wrecking the place again!"

Ursula, on the other hand, *was* terrified. As soon as the trapped strip of her gown ripped free of the wreckage, she took to the air again, screaming, "I'll get you for this, Gustav Gloom!"

Her long gown, sailing behind her like a banner, proved as irresistible to the tyrannosaur as a bit of ribbon dangled for a playful kitten.

The tyrannosaur clamped his jaw tight on

the trailing end and yanked. Ursula spun toward him, like a yo-yo does after somebody's yanked on its string. The yards and yards of silky clothes swirled around her as she spun, screaming, toward the tyrannosaur's mouth.

He opened wide and chomped.

Then the stairway collapsed underneath him.

Fernie What cowered in one of the side corridors as the debris of a dozen broken staircases shattered against the parlor floor. There was something hypnotic about all the destruction, something that she might have seen as fun if she hadn't been worried about her good friend at the center of it all.

She barely noticed all the shadows rushing past her to escape the disaster, from the elegant ladies in evening gowns and dashing men in tuxedos muttering angrily about the uncouth atmosphere in this establishment to the scruffier types in the shadows of T-shirts and torn jeans who exclaimed, "Whoa! What a great way to end a party!"

Beside her, Hives flinched as one wooden

staircase hit the ground almost whole, then shattered as it struck, sending splinters whirling in every direction. "Oh, dear. I hope nobody's expecting *me* to clean that up."

Emerging from a narrow door behind him, looking tired but triumphant, Gustav Gloom said, "I don't know, Hives. Would you?"

"I'd really prefer not," the terrible butler said.

The next sound was a loud *thud* as two massive clawed feet landed on the tiled floor just outside the passageway, making a pair of craters where they hit. "Gustav? Buddy? You in there?"

Gustav took Fernie by the hand and led her out of the sheltered hallway and into the grand parlor, where she stood blinking through heavy clouds of disturbed dust. Above her, the tyrannosaur struggled in vain to use his tiny forearms to free a long strip of gray silk from between two of his front teeth. There was no Ursula at the strip's end, just a rather nasty-looking rip.

The tyrannosaur spotted her and ceased his exercise in flossing. "You're Fernie What, right?"

"Right," she said, feeling somewhat inappropriately shy at the belated introduction. "And from what I hear, you're Fluffy."

"I don't understand you at all," the tyrannosaur

complained. "Why did you call me twice and then *run* from me both times I came to your rescue? What was the point of Gustav arranging for my help beforehand if you were going to do something foolish like that? Do you know how hard it is for somebody my size to fit into some of those tiny corridors, let alone keep up with somebody who insists on running away and hiding?"

Fernie felt terrible. "I'm sorry, Fluffy. Gustav never bothered to tell me the whistle was for calling *you*. To me it just looked like the whistle wasn't working and some random scary monster was chasing me."

Though Fernie hadn't been able to put a finger on the feeling that nagged at her outside the Hall of Shadow Criminals, it had been the convenience of the dinosaur showing up after the emergency whistle was blown.

He snarled his irritation. "Didn't you hear me say, 'I'm coming to get you, Fernie What'? What did you *think* that meant?"

"I thought you were coming to get me for *lunch*."

The tyrannosaur sniffed. "As if you even smell like something I would eat."

Fernie had felt very silly back at the Gallery

176

of Possible Futures when Gustav finally explained who Fluffy was. The emergency whistle had of course worked perfectly all along, which must have been one reason why the disguised Nebuchadnezzar had seized his opportunity to yank it off Pearlie's neck when they were underwater.

Of course, the whistle couldn't give Fluffy more detailed instructions, such as how to spring a trap for the Four Terrors on the stairwells above the grand parlor. So Gustav had sent Hives with a message about a detailed plan that could only be set in motion when the terrible butler returned from that errand and was able to see to Fernie's safety.

"Anyway," Fluffy told Gustav, "I did what you asked and ate them. I only saw three of them, so that means the fourth is still running around here somewhere, but at least I got those three."

Fernie wondered out loud, "Are they dead?"

"What?" Gustav asked, and then, absorbing her question, shook his head. "Oh, no. I've told you many, many times that it's very, very difficult to kill a shadow. If it weren't, I wouldn't have asked Fluffy here to drop so much heavy wreckage on all the innocents in the grand parlor.

That didn't do much more than inconvenience them. Being eaten by Fluffy won't do much worse to Ursula, Carlin, and Otis."

"They're just stuck in my stomach," Fluffy explained.

Fernie's eyebrows knit. "And that takes care of them forever?"

Gustav and Fluffy shared an embarrassed glance.

"They'll find their way out," Fluffy said after a moment. "But it won't be for a while, and I'm not sure it's nice to talk about exactly how."

Fernie realized that she honestly didn't want to. "Won't we have to deal with them all over again then?"

"Oh, no. When the time comes, I'll be sure to, shall we say, deposit them back in a cage. It shouldn't be a big problem. I've done it before."

Behind them all, Hives sniffed. "On that lovely note, young Master Gustav . . . will that be all?"

"No," Gustav said. "I need you to stay here for a few minutes."

"Very well." Hives turned to leave. "Stay right—"

"I mean," Gustav said hastily, "I'm *ordering* you to stay here."

The terrible butler returned, rolling his eyes in exasperation to show how much he would have preferred to be elsewhere.

Gustav took on the manner of a general detailing the plans for an upcoming battle. "All right. Here's the problem, everybody: We've just done very well getting rid of *most* of our problem, but that only means that Fernie's father and sister are in even more trouble than they were before."

Fernie had a sinking feeling. "Why?"

"Because if Nebuchadnezzar and whoever he's working for ever think that their side is going to lose, even for a moment, they won't wait to lose. They'll just decide to be satisfied with what they already have and throw Pearlie and Mr. What into the Pit while they still can. So we can't afford to march in with superior numbers. Fernie and I have to go alone so they still think they can win."

Fluffy's face wasn't able to form many facial expressions as he didn't have any eyebrows, and any attempt to smile or frown just worked out to more ways for a tyrannosaur to look hungry. But he did manage to look concerned now. "Doesn't that mean *actually* making it possible for them to win?"

"Yes," Gustav said. "It does mean that."

The swift defeat of Ursula and the others had left Fernie hoping that the worst was over; now she knew that the worst was yet to come, and felt a chill that penetrated to her bones.

Fluffy still didn't get the point. "So the plan is for the two of you to walk in alone, and for them to think they're winning, and then for Hives and me to rush in like the cavalry and beat them up?"

"No," Gustav said. "That *can't* be the plan. Because, again, if they ever believe that there's even a slight chance of that happening, they lose all reason to not throw Pearlie and Mr. What into the Pit now. They have to know, know and *trust*, that we've left all help behind. They have to know, know and *trust*, that we're coming alone and not planning any tricks."

Fluffy stomped his foot. "But I *have* to be able to help!"

"You can. Just not the way you hoped." Gustav turned to Fernie. "May I have the whistle, please?"

Fernie silently handed it to Gustav.

He held it out to Fluffy. "Please. In the name of our friendship, take this to the farthest possible part of the house. Hide it somewhere I'll never find it. Promise me now, loudly enough for every shadow in this house to hear, that you'll never answer any distress signal from this whistle ever again."

Fluffy hesitated, then lowered his massive face to Gustav's outstretched hand and lapped up the whistle with a tongue the size of a car door. Then he straightened up and let out one of the mightiest roars Fernie had ever heard, a roar that shook the rafters and brought even more debris from the damaged staircases high above tumbling to the parlor floor. "HEAR ME, ALL SHADOWS WHO ROAM THESE HALLS, WHETHER FRIEND OR FOE OR POWERS IN BETWEEN! I, FLUFFY, THE SHADOW OF THE MIGHTIEST PREDATOR TO EVER WALK THIS EARTH, HEREBY PROMISE THAT THIS WHISTLE WILL NEVER AGAIN SUMMON ME TO THE AID OF MY GOOD FRIEND GUSTAV GLOOM! I MAKE THIS SOLEMN VOW IN THE NAME OF ALL THE BEASTS WHOSE MEREST FOOTSTEP

ONCE MADE THE GROUND THUNDER! THIS WHISTLE'S CLAIM ON ME IS DEAD!" He closed his mouth, took a deep breath, and then added, "PINKY SWEAR!"

The revelation that dinosaurs had pinky swears, or at least knew what they were despite not having any pinkies of their own, left Fernie wondering anew just how old her dad really was.

But even that did little to defuse the sadness of the moment, as the shadow tyrannosaur lowered his head for a good-bye pat from Gustav before stomping off into the distance toward one of the few open hallways capable of accommodating him.

The thunderous drumbeat of his every step faded into a distant vibration, and then into silence.

Even Hives looked impressed. "And me, young master?"

Gustav turned to him. "Hives, I'm *ordering* you to take a message to Nebuchadnezzar, wherever he hides. You will confirm that he still has Pearlie and Mr. What, and that they are unharmed. If they're okay, you will extract from him his promise that he will hold off on hurting them or throwing them into the Pit until we arrive. In return, you will promise him that Fernie and I will head straight there, without recruiting any further allies, gathering any additional weapons, or making any further plans. You will tell him that all my promises will be kept, in the name of my grandfather Lemuel Gloom, for only as long as he keeps his. Once you have done all this, you will return here to report your success; and then you will take the rest of the night off, and not accept any more orders from anybody, no matter how urgent they might be. Do you have all that?"

Hives clicked his heels. "Yes, sir." He made as if to turn, then hesitated and turned back. "May I say before I go, sir, that serving your family all these years, as unpleasant and thoroughly beneath me as it has been, has not been quite as completely horrible an imposition on my time as I've sometimes made it sound?"

Gustav nodded. "That's the nicest thing you've ever said to me, Hives."

The terrible butler turned his back and drifted away, picking up speed as he went.

The constant shadow conversation that always filled the grand parlor, and the clattering of smaller debris that still echoed across the tile floor and rebounded off the walls all seemed to stop at once, as if the whole world had just taken a deep breath.

Fernie had the impression that Gustav had just done something irrevocable, something that could never, ever be undone. "What are we going to do?"

He brushed a mote of dust off the bridge of his nose. "Lose, probably."

"That's not funny."

"It's not supposed to be. It just is. Whenever you find yourself having to do something terribly dangerous against impossible odds, you always go in knowing that you're probably going to lose. And you know what?"

"What?"

"We're already ahead of the game. We saved the world once. Not many people can say that. And we did it as best friends. Not many people can say that, either."

He walked over to one of the parlor's many plush sofas, brushed aside some of the dust that had fallen from above, and sat down to pick some of the other debris off the soles of his stocking feet.

Fernie waited for him to say more, realized

that no more was forthcoming, and then ventured to the couch opposite his. The hubbub of shadows in conversation resumed. The gray mist that covered the floor of most places in the Gloom mansion drifted past them like a river that didn't care one bit how long the two friends sat there, or what happened to them.

For ten minutes, she unsuccessfully fought tears. He dusted off his ruined suit. Neither one of them said as much as a single word.

Then Hives returned. "It's all arranged, young master."

"Thank you," said Gustav. He hopped off the couch and then extended a hand to Fernie. "Ready?"

Fernie had used up her tears, exactly as Gustav had probably planned.

"Ready," she said. "Let's go kick their butts."

CHAPTER FOURTEEN
THE MOST FRIGHTENING THING GUSTAV COULD POSSIBLY DO

Fernie had been to the Pit room before and found it a terrible place: a dusty, dank basement room ringed with doors and dominated at its center by a circular black hole, filled to the brim with churning shadow-stuff.

For shadows, it was a swift route to the Dark Country where all their kind came from. They could come and go as they pleased, and considered the trip just a matter of getting from here to there. But the journey was reported to be very different for human beings who fell into the Pit.

Human beings tumbled head over heels for a terribly long time, so very long that they stopped believing that they'd ever reach the bottom. When they finally landed, it was in the darkest, strangest, most terrible place they'd ever been, where they wandered lost and alone until, more often than not, Lord Obsidian came to claim them as his own.

Only love for her family and trust in Gustav could have persuaded Fernie to face that terrible fate a second time.

They went down stairs, through hidden passages, into darkened hallways, and into even stranger places, descending into parts of the house that felt darker and colder and ever more ominous.

Then they turned a corner into a section of corridor so dark that its single flickering candlestick only created a small bubble of light next to an open door, where they saw the shadow of a familiar little girl holding a red balloon on a string.

The little girl spoke in a nasty adult voice, hoarse and whispery, in the manner some very old women attain only after living long lives filled with cruelty and malice. "Hello. Like my balloon?"

It looked like the same red balloon from the room where Fernie had last seen her sister.

Gustav said, "I don't suppose there's helium in there."

"Oh, no," Nebuchadnezzar sang. "Of course not. What use have I for helium? No, I've been amusing myself capturing some of the house's more helpless shadows as tributes for my new master. This balloon has a number of shadow cats, shadow mice, and even a few other inconsequential shadow creatures in it, all trapped together so I can bring them down to the Dark Country to join Lord Obsidian's unwilling army. Oh, and Fernie? It also has your sister's shadow, and your father's; I wouldn't want the likes of them getting loose and causing trouble before our big moment together. Now that you've come to surrender yourselves, I'd also take your shadows as a precaution, but"—the little girl looked down—"I see that neither of you has a shadow at present. I do hope this is not some kind of juvenile trick."

Gustav shook his head. "I don't know where Fernie's shadow is. She's been missing for a while. Mine I haven't seen since the prison break. I'm not about to pull him out of my pocket, either."

The little girl's face puckered, becoming the visage of a very old, very evil woman, horribly out of place on the childlike body. Now Nebuchadnezzar spoke in a child's voice: the kind of voice that only very nasty, very mean-spirited children attain when their chief pleasure in life is making other children cry. "You're up to something."

"I am," said Gustav, as if astonished that Nebuchadnezzar hadn't figured this out yet.

"Your insufferable butler said there'd be no tricks!"

"My *terrible* butler," Gustav corrected, "would have said exactly what he was ordered to say. You should ask yourself: *Do* I know where Fernie's shadow is? The answer's no. Am I holding out hope that my shadow will still catch up with us? The answer's no. Did I order Hives to take the rest of the night off? The answer's yes. Did I send Fluffy away with the emergency whistle? The answer to that's yes, too. Did I promise to surrender without a fight and not even try to win? That I never said. And neither did Fernie."

Nebuchadnezzar transformed his face into that of a battle-scarred, ancient warrior, with a pug nose, sharp cheekbones, and sneering lips. "What *are* you planning?"

"I also never promised to answer your stupid questions."

Fernie, wanting to say something equally impressive, appropriated a line a hero had spoken in one of her favorite books: "Now give my family back, you foul villain, or face my infinite wrath."

This turned out to be far more effective than she ever would have dared hope. For just a moment, Nebuchadnezzar looked just as unnerved as the bad guy in that old book had been.

Then a soft, terribly familiar, terribly evil chuckle emerged from the open doorway, followed by the sound of one man applauding. Each clap was as loud as a gunshot, as ominous as a coffin lid swinging shut. There was a terrible confidence to that applause, an absolute certainty that even if Gustav and Fernie had a plan in mind, it could not possibly deter the forces that stood against them. With a terrible chill in the back of her neck, Fernie suddenly knew who would emerge from that doorway, who had arranged the prison break, and who had been commanding the Four Terrors all along. She had to fight the urge to run for her life.

A voice like boots crunching on broken glass intoned, "You have become very fffffearsome . . . Ffffernie."

The owner of that voice stepped from the doorway.

He was tall, skeletally thin, and paler even than Gustav . . . with bloodred eyes and a leering grin that suggested any number of terrible, cruel jokes played on innocents unlucky enough to fall within his reach. He wore a black suit with a long swirling cape and a chimney of a top hat with a bend in the middle that might have been a tribute to the twisted brain beneath it, or evidence of some ineffective fight put up by one of his previous victims.

He was not a shadow but a man . . . a man who had, to use his own word, *taken* any number of poor innocent people for his own cruel amusement before turning his dark talents to Lord Obsidian's service.

She now understood who had pulled the unconscious Pearlie into that hidden passage during her own last confrontation with Nebuchadnezzar. She had been only a few feet away from the People Taker then, almost close enough for him to step out of the darkness and grab her; but he already had Pearlie to take care of, and confidence that Fernie and Gustav would go exactly where he wanted them to go, anyway.

Nebuchadnezzar, who had seemed such a powerful, threatening figure all on his own just a few seconds before, seemed to shrink in the presence of his employer, as if afraid of being struck. "I was about to bring them to you."

"Oh," the People Taker said, giving the suddenly meek Nebuchadnezzar an affectionate pat on the head, "I know, my new friend. You might have been willing to dissssssobey me, but not the lord we both serve. Hello, Gussssstav. Hello, Ffffffernie. Ssssssurprised to sssssee me so ssssssoon?"

"Not even remotely," Gustav said with unnerving calm. "I expected you."

"You're lying."

"Nope. It was obvious. I could understand Nebuchadnezzar here deciding that he didn't like Fernie for some reason—they seem to have some history together I don't know about—but you were the only person we've met who would have a grudge against her entire family and make a point of wanting them all to fall into the Pit at the same time. Fernie, Pearlie, their dad's shadow, and even their cat, Harrington, all joined together with me to knock you into the Pit the last time you showed your ugly head. You want them to fall together because together they made you fall. Right?"

The People Taker clapped his hands together in glee. "You *are* a clever boy!"

"I suppose your master, Lord Obsidian, said it was okay to take your revenge on the Whats as long as you also did what you were really sent back up here to do: recruit the Four Terrors for his army."

"He must have needed some more servants," Fernie said. "He couldn't have been all that happy with the job you were doing after you were defeated by three kids and a cat."

The People Taker's confident leer faltered a little. "You will pay for that insult, Ffffffernie."

She forced herself to shrug. "Whatever. You are *so* boring."

It was a wonder the People Taker didn't rush across the hallway and attack her right away. But then his rage vanished, replaced with that same terrible confidence he'd shown before, and he stepped away from the doorway, inviting her in with an exaggerated bow and flourish. "You misjudge me, Ffffffernie. I think you will fffffind the game I have planned for your fffffamily . . . mossssst *interesting*."

She did not want to take him up on the invitation. But then Gustav gave her hand a reassuring squeeze, letting her know that all was not yet lost, and she considered the price of letting the People Taker, or his minion Nebuchadnezzar, know how cold and without hope her heart had just turned in her chest. So she raised her head high, released Gustav's hand, and walked alone through the open doorway, too proud to give either villain so much as a second look.

The Pit room was every bit as gray and forbidding as it had been on her last unwilling visit. If anything it was darker, the shadow-stuff in the Pit brimming over as if there was some violent storm in the country far below. But there had been some additions, key among them the two long wooden planks that had been placed over the Pit itself, held in place only by the foot or so each end extended over the sides.

Each plank bore a single unconscious figure. Their balance was so precarious that they clearly remained on the planks for only as long as they could be trusted not to roll over in their sleep or panic upon waking.

Mr. What lay on his back, snoring, a thin line of drool trickling out of the right corner of his mouth. His left foot had slipped off the edge, and his shoe had dangled from his foot, remaining in place only because it had not yet slid off his big toe. Pearlie lay on her side, her mouth curled in a smile while her left arm dangled off the board and swung, just the slightest bit, from whatever unearthly currents stirred beneath the surface of the mist.

Fernie almost rushed to their aid, but Gustav stopped her with a sharp *"Fernie! Don't!"*

She froze and looked behind her. Gustav had entered the room and, sizing up the situation faster than she had, cried out to stop her from making what would have been a terrible mistake.

He calmed down now that she'd listened to him and not rushed forward. As she watched, he stepped away from the entrance to the room and circled the Pit, keeping his distance from it, and from her. Behind him, the People Taker swept into the room with a flourish, but made no attempt to seize Gustav or chase Fernie right away; instead, he stepped aside, watching the scene before him with deep, vicious amusement. Nebuchadnezzar bobbed along behind him, still clutching the red balloon, his face shifting with every heartbeat to form ever newer portraits of the mean and cruel.

"Vvvvvery ssssssmart," the People Taker crowed. "I'd worried that the ssssilly girl would make the obvious mistake right away and deprive me of my game."

Fernie's hands curled into fists. "What game?"

"The game that will make thisssss a little bit more than just an exercise in throwing you in. I thought you children deserved the heartache of fffffailing sssssspectacularly, after all the humiliation you caused me last time. So I cut those planks myself. Each of them is jusssssst thick enough, and therefore sssssstrong enough, to ssssupport the weight of the one person lying on it. Each one will brrrrreak in the middle if you try to add your own weight . . . which means that you won't be able to crawl out on your hands and knees to pull either one to sssssafety."

Fernie felt sickened as she imagined what it would be like to crawl out onto her sister's plank and hear it start to crack in the middle.

The People Taker grinned more widely, enjoying her heartbroken misery the way a fan of ice cream would enjoy two scoops of pistachio with sprinkles. "Of course, you can go another way. You can plant yourself on solid ground, grab one end of a plank, and try to pull it toward you. But as soon as the other end sssssslips off the edge, that plank will dip, just the sssssslightest bit, and your loved one will sssssslide, sssssslide, sssssslide down into the darkness."

Fernie shouted, "You're evil!"

"Thank you. I try so hard to be. Of course, sssssince there are two of you here, you may attempt to sssssave your loved ones with teamwork. Working together, you can grab a plank by both ends at once and sssssslide it sideways, hoping you can keep its passenger balanced for however long it takes you to move the plank to sssssafety. Of course, all that jostling will probably make the plank's passenger rrrrroll off . . . and while you're busy doing that, you will also have to defend yourselves from me. Sssssstill, you might get lucky. If you're very, very careful, you might be able to sssssave your sister, at least. I'm not entirely sure that even children your size who've eaten all their green beans will be able to manage a sssssufficiently smooth ride to save your fffffather."

Fernie hated to admit it, but the People Taker was right. As strong as she was, and as strong as Gustav was, it was impossible to imagine the two of them managing to not only lift but gently carry the plank bearing her father to safety.

"Of course," the People Taker said, "if you remain too fffffrightened of what mmmmmight happen to do anything within the next fffffew minutes, your fffffather and ssssssister will ssssstart to wake up and move around . . . and they'll ssssolve your problem by fffffalling in even without your bungling help."

Fernie circled the Pit, her heart pounding as she searched for some possible answer. Gustav circled on the other side, his eyebrows knitting as he also regarded the problem from every angle.

"Plusssss," the People Taker concluded, "the ssssssecond I sssssee you start to try anything, it becomes my pleasure, and Nebuchadnezzar's, to ssssstop you. How are you going to manage *this* miracle? *How* are the two of you going to fffffight me, when I see you're both missing your shadows, and last time we fffffought you only barely defeated me when you also had your ssssssister's help *and* the help of all your shadows *and* that ssssstupid cat of yours?"

Fernie had no ideas.

On the other side of the Pit, Gustav had

crouched to examine the situation from close up, while rubbing his chin in what looked like deep concentration. But now he stood up and gave her infinite hope by *winking* at her, letting her know that all was not yet lost.

Then he faced the People Taker and said, "I've got to hand it to you. All you had to work with was a Pit and a pair of planks, and you came up with a truly classic death trap."

"Thank you." The People Taker beamed like a pastry chef complimented on the quality of his blueberry muffins. "I'm *ssssso* glad you like it."

Gustav blinked. "I didn't say I liked it."

"I'm not *sssssurprised*. Nobody likes being beaten."

"I didn't say I was beaten, either. You see, I don't like bullies. I don't like people making games out of hurting others, and I don't like you coming back into my house causing more trouble when we all did a perfectly acceptable job of getting rid of you once before. Most of all, you silly, silly person, I don't like you thinking that I entered this room unprepared and capable of being stopped by a simple little problem like this, when my good friend here just finished telling me a little while ago that she *believes in me*."

For a fraction of a second, the People Taker didn't look quite as much like the unstoppable force of nature he usually was . . . but like a pale, unnerved ghost of a man, recognizing in the face of an enemy a force far more powerful than himself.

In the second it took him to recover his composure and replenish the menace dripping from his smile, Nebuchadnezzar changed shapes from a scowling old woman to a leering skeleton in robes and spoke for him. "You're bluffing."

"Try again," said Gustav.

Reaching into his jacket pocket, he did something he almost never did; something that, at this particular moment, was likely the most frightening thing he could have done.

He smiled.

CHAPTER FIFTEEN
"NERTS"

Gustav's hand emerged from his jacket pocket with a whistle in it.

Nebuchadnezzar gasped in horror. "You said you sent your dinosaur away with the whistle!"

"With *that* whistle," Gustav said. "You were supposed to believe that it was the only one. I have a whole drawer full of them, and they *all* call Fluffy."

He tossed the whistle over his shoulder to Fernie, who caught it in the air.

Then he took another out of his pocket.

"See?" he said. "I have plenty. I always keep my pockets filled with them in case I lose one."

The People Taker's grin returned. "Vvvvvery clever, boy. But as master plans go, it's not that impressive. Fffffrom what I've observed tonight, it always takes your pet dinosaur several minutes to arrive. You could blow that whistle now and

I'll sssstill have more than enough time to toss the Whats into the Pit."

"I'm certain," Gustav conceded, putting his whistle back in his pocket, "that if that were all I had in mind, I'd be in a lot of trouble now. But it's not. We probably won't even need the dinosaur whistles, because you have a couple of other surprises coming. For instance, remember when I said that I wasn't holding out hope that my shadow would catch up with us? That's because I didn't have to hold out hope. He's already here."

This was news to Fernie. She looked around, searching the room's many dark places for signs of movement, but saw nothing. Nor was she the only person it baffled; the People Taker was also glancing to and fro, looking considerably less confident than he had even a moment earlier.

"I don't see him anywhere," Nebuchadnezzar offered.

"Then *find him!*" the People Taker snapped, just a little bit more loudly than he had to.

Once again cowering as if expecting to be hit, Nebuchadnezzar began to glide around the room, checking every dark place, poking around in every nook. The red balloon bobbed along with him, scraping dust off the ceiling whenever he flew too high. At one point, when he drew close to Fernie and sniffed around her to confirm that she wasn't carrying Gustav's shadow on her person, the latex of that red balloon bulged for just a moment in the shape of her father's face—actually, she corrected herself, in the shape of her father's *shadow's* face. He appeared to be shouting something she couldn't hear. Probably *let me out*.

Unfortunately, she did not have a pin. But she understood that by keeping the People Taker occupied with clever talk, Gustav was giving her a chance to do something.

She considered blowing the extra whistle Gustav had tossed her. It was tempting to believe she could solve everything by just dumping the whole problem in the tyrannosaur's stubby hands. But Gustav hadn't blown the whistle when he had a chance, and after a moment of consideration, she saw why. The last thing she could afford to do, while her father and sister were so precariously balanced on their planks, was anything that made the floors shake. The whistle could only be a backup plan, to be saved until there was no other choice.

She inched to the edge of the Pit and knelt at the base of the plank bearing her unconscious sister. Pearlie seemed closer to waking up than their father; even as Fernie watched, her sister licked her lips, swallowed, and fell into a doze again, her dangling arm continuing to stir the shadow-stuff in lazy circles.

Emerging from under a set of three stairs leading to one of the room's four exit doors, and dragging the remains of a cobweb as well as the leashed balloon behind him, Nebuchadnezzar exploded with curses. "I don't see the boy's shadow anywhere!"

"And yet," Gustav said, "somehow the two of you both know I'm not lying."

The People Taker grimaced. "I believe that's the lassssst ssssstraw . . ."

During their prior encounter, Fernie had been astounded by just how quickly the People Taker could move when he wanted to, and had almost forgotten that terrible speed in light of all the strange shadow-magic she'd seen since. But he demonstrated his terrible swiftness again now, disappearing from the spot where he'd been standing and appearing, almost without so much as a blur, within grabbing range of Gustav.

At least, he appeared within grabbing range of *where Gustav had been*.

But even as the People Taker's hands clutched empty air, Gustav appeared on his shoulders, neatly plucking the bent top hat off his head and leaping away with it in his hands.

"Come back with that!" the People Taker roared.

"I'm almost sorry I took it!" Gustav noted. "Don't you ever wash your hair?"

Bellowing, the People Taker gave chase. Fernie had never seen a grown man run so fast—it was almost impossible to make out his movements, only the blurs and brief little impressions of his terrible form whenever he slowed down for another grab at Gustav. She caught a glimpse of him clutching for her friend, of her friend diving between the People Taker's knees, of the two of them leaping past each other in midair, of the black cape slashing to and fro like the wings of some furious bird. There was nothing Fernie could do to get in the middle of that. She could only try to help Pearlie and their father while the People Taker was distracted.

The only problem was, she still had no idea what to do.

She knelt by the end of the plank bearing Pearlie and felt her heart almost burst from her chest when her big sister suddenly moved.

Pearlie pulled her arm back up to her chest, then seemed to realize that something was terribly wrong and groped at the empty space beside her, feeling nothing.

Fernie cried out. "Pearlie! Don't move an inch!"

Pearlie twitched and came very close to rolling over the side, but suddenly froze as she registered the narrowness of her wooden bed and the terrible unsettling emptiness beneath it. Without even opening her eyes, she said, "Oh, nerts. We're still in Gustav's house, aren't we?"

"Yes," Fernie said. "In the Pit room. Whatever you do, don't roll over."

Across the room, a familiar hateful voice cried, "I said, give me back my hat!"

Pearlie stiffened further. "Was that the People Taker? Again?"

"Yes."

"Nerts," Pearlie said, this time with feeling. "I really hate that guy."

Across the room, Gustav leaped off one of

the short sets of stairs, kicked off the wall just ahead of the People Taker's clutching fingers, and seized the red balloon from the end of Nebuchadnezzar's string. A stunning pop, somehow louder than the mere sound it made, filled the room as he burst it with his fingers in midair.

A hundred tiny spots of darkness exploded in all directions, expanding to become the shadows Nebuchadnezzar had taken captive: shadow dogs, shadow cats, shadow insects, and all manner of stranger creatures, tumbling to the stone floor and fleeing for cover from the battle taking place around them. The two largest freed shadows belonged to Pearlie and Mr. What, bobbing about in too much of a daze to react as quickly as the lower animals.

The flesh-and-blood Pearlie almost jumped out of her skin when she heard the pop, and almost fell over the side of her plank. She squealed, clamped her knees tight, and pulled herself back on top with her hands, hugging the wood with a desperation that looked like she would have been perfectly happy to just hold on tight and not make any further attempt to crawl to safety.

"Don't open your eyes," Fernie advised. "Just guide yourself along with your hands and pull yourself to me."

Even as Pearlie inched along, freezing again with every slight movement of her plank, the People Taker saw that at least one of his victims was now trying to save herself. He abandoned his pursuit of Gustav and charged the Pit, screaming, drawing back one leg for a kick that would have sent plank and girl plummeting into the Dark Country.

Two dark blurs, the shadows of Pearlie and Mr. What, tackled him at the shoulders, landing with absolutely no weight and not at all slowing him down. Gustav tackled the leg the People Taker had planted on the floor and had better effect. The People Taker fell over, boy and man disappearing under the same billowing cloak.

There was no way to tell what was happening under that cloak, but it was angry and it was violent. The People Taker cried out in sudden pain. A punch landed in somebody's stomach. Gustav gasped. The cloak billowed up and down like an angry sea disturbed by beasts fighting just below the surface. Nebuchadnezzar, now looking like a wizened old man, hovered low above the fray, looking for a chance to enter it . . . and then was dragged in by his ankle by a shadowy gray hand that looked like Mr. What's.

They were all still fighting, only a few steps away, as Pearlie came close enough to the end of her plank for Fernie to pull her to safety. The two sisters embraced, just for a second—and might have hugged for much longer than that had Pearlie not opened her eyes for the first time during the ordeal and seen their father still precariously balanced on his own plank.

"Oh, no! Dad!"

"He's next," declared Fernie, who immediately jumped up and started pulling Pearlie's plank to safety on her side of the Pit.

Several feet away, the snarling People Taker managed to stand, despite the several shadows and squirming boy still clinging to him. It was no surprise that their combined efforts would not be enough to stop him, since a much greater weight of struggling children and motivated shadows had barely slowed him down the last time he and the kids had fought a dire battle in this room. He peeled Gustav off his shoulders and held him at arm's length by the collar, leering at the boy's ineffective punches. He glanced at the Pit, where the girls were running around the far side carrying the now-unoccupied plank. With supreme disdain he addressed his servant: "Oh, Nebuchadnezzar? I'm bored with my game. Do make sure their fffffather falls in."

Nebuchadnezzar tore himself away from Mr. What's shadow and assumed what might have been his true shape, a runny-faced goblin with fiery eyes and a fang-lined, twisted mouth, but there was still something terribly childlike about him, as if he'd become the monster he was at a very young age and had never grown out of it.

There was no way to stop him from planting both his feet on Mr. What's chest and howling in the voice of the fake little girl Fernie had rejected. "You should have accepted my friendship, Fernie!"

He raised both arms high above his head, displaying hands that had become more like claws, with nails that ended in barbed hooks.

Fernie cried out as those barbed hooks came down.

But Nebuchadnezzar's claws never came close to touching Mr. What.

A patch of darkness scrambled out of Mr. What's shirt pocket, unfolded into the shape of a boy, seized Nebuchadnezzar by the wrists, and drove him into the air.

It was Gustav's shadow.

Fernie suddenly remembered: Gustav had told Nebuchadnezzar that he wasn't about to pull the shadow out of his pocket—but he hadn't said anything about Mr. What's.

On their trip through the Hall of Shadow Criminals, even before the prison break began, he must have taken this extra precaution to make sure Mr. What remained safe. His shadow had been hiding on Mr. What ever since, waiting for the most advantageous moment to jump out and act.

Gustav's shadow began wrestling with Nebuchadnezzar in midair but was having trouble with him, because he was limited to the form of a boy and the shape-changer was building up his arms to make them stronger and bulkier and more like the arms of a giant. The two slashed and punched and kicked at each other, but Nebuchadnezzar was clearly stronger, clearly more savage and dangerous; whatever damage shadows in battle were capable of doing to each other, Nebuchadnezzar was surely ready to deliver more.

"Fernie!" Gustav's shadow shouted. "Save your dad while you have a chance!"

Across the room, the People Taker hurled Gustav to the ground, then—showing his disdain for his enemies with his lack of any particular hurry—reached down to pick up his fallen hat. Though stunned by his fall, Gustav still managed to kick it away. The hat rolled across the room, and the People Taker shrieked, momentarily more concerned with his headwear than with either the girls or their father. He darted for it, but Pearlie's shadow snatched it up and tossed it overhand to Mr. What's shadow, who tossed it back, the furious People Taker leaping first one way and then the next in momentary utter distraction from the job he was here to do.

Over at the Pit, Fernie took the rescued plank from Pearlie, put it down by her side, and knelt down at the side of the Pit nearest her dad's feet. She confirmed that the plank he rested on was longer than the diameter of the Pit by about two feet, with an equal amount resting on each edge of the Pit.

"Quick, weigh down the end nearest his head!"

Pearlie didn't ask any questions. She ran

around the Pit again and dropped down onto her knees, resting all her weight on the end of her father's plank.

Above them both, Gustav's shadow clung to Nebuchadnezzar, trying to prevent those terrible sickle arms from slashing downward. Nebuchadnezzar shifted shape again, and a tail started to emerge from his back—an awful, segmented shape, like a scorpion's stinger.

Below, Fernie carried the other plank a third of the way around the Pit and lowered one end into the murk, extending it outward until it passed under the section of her father's plank that bore his outstretched legs. After a moment she pulled it back, reconsidered, and moved closer to the base of the circle, where the two sides of the Pit were only a few feet apart. This time she didn't have to extend her plank too far beneath her father's and was able to reach the stones on the Pit's opposite wall. The other end of the plank she held hit stone only a couple of feet below the rim.

"Pearlie!" she cried again. "Grab the other end!"

Pearlie rushed to help, plopped down on her belly, and reached down with both arms to grab the other end of Fernie's plank. It took her two tries to get it, but she did, securing her grip before pulling her end up.

In the air, the clawed and fanged Nebuchadnezzar whipped his scorpion tail at Gustav's shadow, who avoided the strike by dropping like a stone and grabbing hold of the other shadow's ankles as he went. Nebuchadnezzar hadn't expected this. Both shadows fell into the Pit, disappearing below the surface murk.

Across the room, the People Taker leaped up and snatched his hat out of midair, placing it very firmly on his head and even adjusting it to the proper angle before glancing at the Pit and seeing the two What girls working together to rescue their father. This infuriated him. He spun with a twirl of his cape, driving back the two shadows and one boy in the act of charging him again, and stormed toward the girls, screaming, "You're not going to get away with it this time, you little brats!"

Gustav and the shadows of Pearlie and Mr. What were close behind him and catching up, but in that second, there was no doubt. The People Taker would get to Fernie and Pearlie and Mr. What first.

And yet Gustav hadn't lied before when he'd told the People Taker that the extra whistle and his own hiding shadow weren't the only surprises he'd prepared. Another, as startling as the rest put together, now stormed into the room wearing a scowl of pure rage and placed himself in the People Taker's path.

Fernie gasped when she saw who it was. "*Hives?!* But you're supposed to be a terrible butler! You're not supposed to help anybody unless they order you to!"

Hives hammered the People Taker with flurries of angry blows. "That's my job description, miss! But why else do you think Gustav made such a point of giving me the night off? When I'm on my own time, I can do anything I want! *And I want to help my friend Gustav!*"

The girls now had a few seconds to complete their own critical job. The extra plank now bridged the Pit underneath the one holding Mr. What, bracing it at a right angle, like a cross. Mr. What's plank had angled upward by an inch when the other one was slipped under it . . . but his delicate balance had held.

His own plank didn't tip at all as the two straining girls pulled it toward safety.

Unfortunately, the jarring woke him up. His eyes shot open, and he instinctively sat up on his plank—just in time for the jarring to unbalance him completely. His arms spun like the blades of a windmill, fighting for balance. One leg shot up, the other slipped off the side of his plank, and he yelled, "Fernie! Pearlie!"

Nebuchadnezzar's head popped up above the Pit's murk. Whatever had happened between him and Gustav's shadow in the last few seconds, he no longer wore a scorpion tail, but was just an innocent-looking little girl again, one who flashed the sweetest and cutest little smile as he launched himself at Mr. What's back.

The arms of Gustav's shadow reached up through the murk and dragged him back down into darkness.

As the murk bubbled from the epic battle taking place below, Mr. What slipped off the side of his plank, his legs disappearing into shadow-stuff. He grabbed hold with his arms, pulling himself up on his stomach, but the force of his struggle made the plank dip toward darkness and pulled both of his girls closer to the edge. They screamed at him to hold on, but he saw the trouble they were in on his behalf and instinctively did the only thing a father could do: let go, so his daughters would have a chance at life. He started to slide down the length of the plank toward an endless fall.

Pearlie and Fernie both screamed, "DADDY!"

Gustav's shadow slammed against the underside of the plank, not just righting it but driving it a few feet into the air. Mr. What bounced into the air a few feet above it and landed straddling the plank again. Judging from the sound he made and the expression on his face, it was not the most pleasant experience of his day. Still, he was able to muster enough strength to begin to pull himself along toward his daughters.

Gustav's shadow disappeared beneath the surface again, and the sounds of two shadows in furious battle resumed.

Across the room, the People Taker reeled from punch after punch from Hives's angry fists, landing with actual force against his pale, hateful face.

"I wasn't always a terrible butler, sir! I used to be a pretty good boxer!"

Fernie and Pearlie pulled their father onto solid ground. He was exhausted and out of breath from his struggles with the plank, but otherwise unhurt, and for a moment would not let go of them, murmuring, "I'm sorry, girls, but we really do have to move . . ."

A few feet away, the People Taker fell back, and Gustav leaped on his shoulders, adding his own small blows to the terrible butler's powerful ones. The tide had turned, three shadows and one very strange, very determined boy seemingly seconds from driving the terrible taker of people to his knees. Then Hives fell back, gasping, eyes bugging with the realization that the People Taker had somehow managed to hurt him . . . and Gustav fell to the ground, also hurt, for the moment too out of breath to fight back.

The People Taker screamed in fury and knee-walked over to Gustav's side, joining his fists together high above his head in preparation for a final attack on the boy he now seemed determined to slay with a single blow. Mr. What's shadow and Pearlie's shadow instantly wrapped themselves around his arms, trying to hold them back, but it was clear that even between them, they didn't have the strength to even slow down what was about to happen; and Gustav was too dazed, for the moment, to get out of the way.

The People Taker did not hear the two What girls racing toward him from behind.

They ran side by side, each carrying one end of the long plank that had until a few seconds earlier held their father over the Pit, the plank forming what amounted to a solid wall between them.

On the floor, Gustav saw what was about to happen and looked away.

The People Taker must have thought that Gustav was flinching from the blow he was about to receive. But enough of a twinkle must have shown in Gustav's eyes to warn the People Taker that something very unfortunate was about to happen to him. He glanced over his shoulder just in time to see his entire field of vision obscured by a galloping plank. An ugly brown knothole, dead center, must have looked like a furious wasp going for his eyes.

The People Taker cried, "Ffffernie! *Ffffernie!*"

The center of the plank smacked him full in the face and knocked him down.

It didn't knock him *out*, but it knocked him *silly* enough that it took him a second or two to rise to his knees, and even then it was only in time for the same plank to slam him again after the girls turned around and repeated their run in the opposite direction.

This time the impact left a lightning-shaped crack in the plank, radiating from the knothole.

It didn't do much better for the People Taker's face.

He started to rise again, but his body had different ideas. After a moment he just fell flat on his back, knocked into the sleep of the evil.

Exhausted, the two sisters dumped the plank on top of him, the midpoint balanced on his chest and the raised end addressing the ceiling like a seesaw.

In the silence that followed, Pearlie managed, "I don't *ever* want to come back to this room."

"Neither do I," Gustav gasped. He rose on unsteady legs and stumbled forward to hug them both. "By and large, it's less fun than any room in the house, except maybe the Hall of Incredibly Pointless Board Games."

Hearing that, Fernie dropped all her other questions and declared, "Okay, *that* one I'm pretty sure you just made up."

"I'm afraid he didn't," sniffed Hives, who

rejoined them nursing a terribly swollen nose. "You haven't played a boring game of checkers until you've played the one where the red and black pieces get along. They don't even jump one another. They just circle the board and sing."

CHAPTER SIXTEEN
*EXCEPT

And so, for a few seconds at least, it seemed as if they'd all won themselves an uncomplicated happy ending. They'd entered a dangerous place, faced great perils, defeated great villains, and enjoyed a wonderful reunion when it was all done.

None of them realized, quite yet, that happy endings aren't always that easy to come by. Sometimes they insist on being difficult. There are always other problems, and this was particularly true in the Gloom house, where some of the problems went back for years and others were being born every minute.

The first loose end, a small one, announced itself only a few seconds later, when Gustav's shadow popped up from the murk in the Pit, his shadow clothes as ragged and torn from battle as Gustav's own. He glided over to reunite with his boy. "Sorry, everybody. Nebuchadnezzar got away. I chased him as far down as I could, but had to turn back when I realized that we were halfway to the Dark Country and that he was trying to lead me to Lord Obsidian. It's sad, but I think he'll be working for the bad guys for a little while longer."

"That's okay," Gustav said. "If we had to lose Nebuchadnezzar, then at least we captured *this* guy." He toed the unconscious People Taker with one of his stocking feet.

Fernie glanced down at the People Taker, who was still breathing but not moving much, lips snarling from whatever vile dreams people takers experience after being knocked unconscious with boards. A second loose end occurred to her. "What are we going to do with him? Are we supposed to turn him over to the police?"

"I wish we could. He must still be wanted for all his terrible crimes outside the fence. But I'm afraid that Lord Obsidian's given him certain abilities that would prevent any human prison from ever being able to hold him. And we can't put him in the Hall of Shadow Criminals, either, not even if we build a special cell meant for a person instead of a shadow; not after we learned that Lord Obsidian can free prisoners from there anytime he wants. We'll have to come up with something else. And we have to do it before he wakes up, or we'll just have to fight him all over again."

Hives rolled his eyes. "Perhaps we can take him to a chair in the Too Much Sitting Room?"

Fernie winced. She remembered the Too Much Sitting Room, which still struck her as one of the very worst places in the Gloom household, and—for all the terrible things the People Taker had done to too many people—it seemed like too vicious a punishment, even for somebody as evil as him. She said, "That's cruel."

"So's he," pointed out Hives.

"Isn't there someplace you can put him that will hold him for at least a little while, until you can figure out something permanent?"

The terrible butler considered that. "Oh, certainly. There's the Room of Being Delayed Indefinitely, the Patio of Staying Put, and the

Express Elevator to Somewhere Between Floors; none of those places are meant to hold dangerous criminals, but any one of them should be able to keep him out of mischief until we get around to discussing other options. I don't think it'll be much of a problem, young miss. After all, I'm a terrible butler. I'm used to putting people through endless inconvenience."

Fernie shuddered. "I sure wouldn't want to go to the Room of Being Delayed Indefinitely."

Hives allowed himself the slightest bit of a smile. "It's one of my favorites, young miss."

Behind them, Mr. What, who was the worst off from their shared ordeal, stood leaning against one of the stone walls, catching his breath. "It does sound like your kind of place, Hives."

"Thank you, sir."

Mr. What shook his head, gathered up his strength, and began to shuffle toward them, following a curlicue of a route that crossed itself at several points and came perilously close to the edge of the Pit he had so narrowly escaped. He muttered something about nobody ever listening to him about safety railings and changed direction to join his daughters. Then he stumbled over his own feet and lurched forward, taking a step that ended with his foot coming down on the raised end of the plank on the People Taker's chest.

The third loose end to make itself known in just the last couple of minutes announced itself when the other end of the board shot up and smacked him hard in the face.

"Ow!" he cried, stumbling backward.

It was almost funny until Fernie saw him back up against the Pit, his arms flailing, the heels of his shoes teetering on the edge.

Pearlie, who was closest to him, yelled, "Dad!" and rushed to help him.

She was just fast enough to seize him by the wrist.

He was grateful enough to grasp her with his other hand.

For a heartbeat, it looked like she would succeed in pulling him back.

Instead, she was pulled in when he fell.

It happened so quickly that there was nothing anybody in the room could do. Fernie's father and sister tumbled screaming into darkness, their cries audible far longer than they would have been if they were only traveling a real-world distance. And then those cries were echoed by the screams of the two shadows who belonged to those two people, who flew past Fernie and Gustav and Hives and also dove into the Pit, chasing their lost people into the world where only shadows are meant to live.

Fernie's blood went cold. For almost a full second she refused to accept what she had just seen. Then the terrible nightmare of it all came crashing down on her. She screamed and went after them, ready to jump into the Pit if she had to, not making any more detailed plan than that; only knowing that her family had disappeared before her eyes and she could not let them go without at least trying to save them.

Gustav brought her down with a tackle. "Fernie, don't!"

She fought to free herself. "Let me go! Don't you see? We have to go after them!"

She expected his next words to be a protest that they couldn't, that her father and sister were already gone, but instead he cried, "And we will! I promise! Don't you remember? I was going down there anyway, to save my own dad! I'll save yours, too! But this is not the way! *Lord Obsidian will get you if you go that way!*"

Furious, she hit him a few times, crying that she didn't care, but her punches grew weaker, and she was finally left sobbing like a baby in his arms. He could only say, "We'll get them back, Fernie, we will, we will, we will." He promised her that as soon as he could make the arrangements they would pull off a rescue against overwhelming odds, and her father and sister would be safe.

He promised all this as if there were any way he could possibly be sure.

He almost sounded like he was sure. But she could tell from the hitch in his voice that he was not.

How could he be? The Dark Country was so far away; the forces of Lord Obsidian were still fighting an awful war down there; the journey to that place was nothing any mere boy, even a halfsie boy, should ever be able to accomplish; and even assuming Fernie's father and sister would be found in a place that large, there was still no way she could think of to ever be sure that they could find a way back. Thinking about it, she was once again certain that Gustav was only saying what he knew she wanted to hear. He was lying to her.

"Fernie," he said insistently.

She could barely make out his face through her haze of tears. "What?"

"There's something else. Remember Cousin Cyrus? I sent him to contact Great-Aunt Mellifluous and tell her that your father and sister were in trouble. Once he gets through with that message, they'll have a friend in the Dark Country long before they even get there. That's another thing you can hold on to."

"Cousin Cyrus didn't . . . strike me as the kind of person we can count on."

"He isn't. But I promise you, he always pays his debts. It'll give your father and sister an edge before we show up. And we will show up, Fernie. We'll show up and we'll make it right. I promise you."

It wasn't much. It was just a promise: a promise he really had no business making, because it was not a promise that anybody could make. It was as empty as his promise earlier that a quick errand inside his house would be perfectly safe.

But right now, that promise was all she had.

And he was Gustav Gloom. He had pulled off the impossible before.

More than anything else, she wanted to curl up in a ball and disappear forever. But she had a choice right now: giving up, or believing in her friend. So she wiped her eyes, even though she knew that more tears would be coming before this was done, and she asked:

"How?"

EPILOGUE
WHAT MAKES WINNING POSSIBLE

It took almost an hour for Gustav and Fernie to stir themselves from the scene of Fernie's terrible loss and make their way back to the front door of the Gloom house.

Since there had been no further adventures on the way, the journey might have taken less time, but they needed to stop several times because Fernie kept sitting down every time she thought of the terrible moment she had failed to prevent. Gustav kept telling her that it was going to be okay. He kept saying it so much that it just became background noise, like a radio that's been playing for so long that anybody not actively listening to it forgets that it's on.

There were only the two of them now. Gustav's shadow had gone off to help Hives put the People Taker away in the Room of Being Delayed Indefinitely. Fernie's own shadow remained missing, and that was yet another loss; the shadow girl was not just a part of Fernie herself, but had in some strange way also started to become a friend, and having to worry about her was yet another burden on top of many that were terribly hard to bear. Pearlie's and Mr. What's shadows had both followed their people into the Pit and showed no sign of returning any time soon. Fluffy was wherever he'd gone to "deposit" the other members of the Four Terrors. There were other shadows all about, many skulking around quietly as if wanting to maintain a decent silence in light of what had happened, but they might as well have been a million miles away. The Gloom house still felt very large and very empty, less like a place with life in it than it ever had.

By the time they reached the door, Fernie was so lost in her own thoughts that she hadn't said anything for almost an hour, no matter what was said to her, and Gustav expressed worry that she wouldn't be able to do what needed to be done.

"No," she said, surprising them both. Her eyes burned from recent tears, but they were dry now, and didn't hurt nearly as badly as her injured hand. "I can't just go off with you to the

Dark Country. I have to go get Harrington first, so he isn't left in the house by himself without food or water. And I have to leave a note for my mom, so she'll know what happened if . . . if we don't come back."

"You're right," Gustav said. "You should probably do that."

She hesitated. "You are sure about this? That there is some way to get down to the Dark Country and back?"

"My grandfather went down there years ago," Gustav said. "He had to, to make contact with the shadow world. He went and made the deal with them to make this a shadow house. I don't know how he did it, but that's what I wanted to ask Hieronymus Spector about in the first place. We just have more reasons to ask him now, that's all."

"And he did tell you before all this happened, when this was only about your father, that he would only talk to me."

Gustav looked away. "Yes."

"And he didn't say why."

"No. But I think I know why now. I'm afraid it's a terrible reason, Fernie. It's one of the things we're going to have to talk to him about when we see him."

Fernie didn't ask for an explanation. She just took a deep breath, tasting dust, the air of the old house, the livestock smell of Fluffy, her own sadness . . . and maybe, just maybe, behind all of that, the slightest tinge of hope. "Okay. I won't be long. We'll talk to him as soon as I get back."

The front door opened, revealing the misty front yard, and beyond it, the brighter colors of Sunnyside Terrace, with the Fluorescent Salmon house of the Whats looking like a big sparkling fruit on the other side of the street. It seemed more like home than it ever had, but it also seemed a million miles away.

Fernie had a thought that also seemed to come from a place a million miles away: *What if I never see them again?*

It wasn't the kind of thing she had time to think about right now.

But she did have time to remember that Gustav was her friend and that it was just like him to want to protect her. Just to be sure he didn't get any fancy ideas of that kind, she whirled around and pointed an accusing finger at his face. "I'm warning you. You'd better not talk to Hieronymus or go down to the Dark Country without me. I'd better not come back and find out you're already gone. Not even if you think it's for my own good. I'm serious."

"I wouldn't dream of it," said Gustav. "I promise. I won't do anything but start getting things ready. You do what you have to across the street. Take a few hours. I'll be waiting for you when you get back."

Despite everything that had gone wrong in the last few hours, she found that she didn't doubt him at all. He had made mistakes, but he meant his promises. She believed in him, as much as she'd ever believed in the bravery of her mother, or the kindness of her father, or the good heart of her sister. If there was anybody in the world who could take her on the dangerous journey to go and bring them all back alive, it was Gustav Gloom.

And it was that thought, more than any other, that warmed her and kept her from being afraid.

But she still didn't leave, remaining at the threshold just long enough to think one last terrible thought. "Gustav?"

"What?"

"What if his promise to talk to me is just one of Hieronymus's tricks? What if he refuses to answer our questions?"

Gustav's frown grew tighter and fiercer, becoming the look of a boy only a fool would dare try to disappoint.

He said, "Then we'll make him."

That was what Fernie had needed: certainty. And she found that she herself had more than enough of it. "You're right. He'd better not mess with us, not if he knows what's good for him."

"That's the way to think," Gustav said. "We're more than a match for the likes of him."

Impossibly, she found herself smiling. It was a weak smile, more wan than any normally found on Fernie What's face; but it was also her first smile since that terrible moment at the Pit, one that made her realize that there would be many more smiles to come. Maybe, she thought, the ability to find light even when terrible dark things were coming was the strongest weapon of all. Maybe that made winning possible. All she knew was that, despite everything, there was a small part of her that could hardly wait.

Whatever else happened, it was not going to be dull.

"See you soon," said Gustav.

"Real soon," said Fernie.

Then she turned her back and headed home.

ACKNOWLEDGMENTS

You would not now be seeing this book without the persistence of agents extraordinaire Joshua Bilmes and Eddie Schneider of the Jabberwocky Literary Agency. You would not now be reading it in its present form without the input of the members of the South Florida Science Fiction Society Writers' Workshop, a group that includes Brad Aiken, Dave Dunn, Dave Slavin, and Chris Negelein. You would not now be enjoying the same experience free of verbal land mines and other clutter without the ace red pens of copy editor Kate Ritchey and editor Jordan Hamessley. You would not now be *ooh*ing and *aah*ing over the illustrations without the genius of artist Kristen Margiotta. You would not now be holding the divine artifact in your hands without designer Christina Quintero. You might have no idea the book exists without the fine work of publicist Tara Shanahan. You would not now be seeing any books from me at all without the patience, love, and constant encouragement of my beautiful wife, Judi B. Castro. You would not now be seeing a human being with my name and my face were it not for my parents, Saby and Joy Castro.

And thanks to you, my unknown readers. Due to publishing lag time, this third book is being completed before the first has hit shelves. I thank you, from the distant past, for embarking on this journey with us and hope you stick around to see what happens as Gustav and Fernie storm the Dark Country!

GUSTAV GLOOM

AND THE CRYPTIC CAROUSEL